Unbreak Me

C.A. GRIECO

Copyright © 2023 C.A. Grieco

All rights reserved.

ISBN:9798861818759

To my husband,
thank you for having
more faith in me
than I could have
ever had in myself.

This book is about a woman dealing with the aftermath of her brother taking his own life. There are scenes of domestic violence, murder, and drug and alcohol use.

Unbreak Me

Chapter One

Claire

Grief. That's what the doctor called it last night as the world spun out from under me. My throat closing, heart beating in my ears, as the black spots that formed in my vision threatened to pull me under.

Grief. A normal thing people deal with after going through a hard loss. A word that feels way too simple to describe the immense pain ripping through my body.

I glance around the small crowd gathered around me. The June sun beating down on their tear-streaked faces. Their black clothes a drastic contrast to the cloudless blue sky and bright green grass surrounding us.

The man across from me drags his perfectly tailored suit sleeve across his forehead, wiping off a bead of sweat right before it trails down his nose. Yet my lower lip still trembles uncontrollably, stealing most of my attention from the speech being given next to me. I clench my jaw and pray it stops. I know in only a few brief moments; this whole thing will be over.

There are only a few people here, though I expected as much. I won't lie and tell you that my brother was a saint. The drug induced demons ripped their way through the innocent little boy I once knew.

Mr. and Mrs. Shaw stand across from me. Mrs. Shaw wrapped tightly in Mr. Shaw's arms as silent sobs wrack through her small body. Mr. Shaw uses his one hand to rub up and down her back in a failed attempt to soothe her broken heart as he dabs the countless tears running down his own face.

Mr. Shaw had taken Michael under his wing when he was only sixteen. Michael had stolen his wallet, spending every penny on his next fix. Instead of having him thrown in jail, he got him enrolled in an amazing rehab. Once he got clean, he gave him a job at his roofing company.

Michael spent so many days after that at the Shaw's house. They treated him like their son and constantly told me how much they loved him. Mrs. Shaw had pulled me to the side a few years back. She told me she had prayed for a child. She never knew why that prayer had been left unanswered as old age took root, but when Michael came into their life, she felt like she understood it all.

For years, I thought everything was going great. Michael had stayed out of trouble. He was finally happy.

That's until he met his girlfriend, May. The first time I caught them together was after he had disappeared for two weeks without warning. I knew she was nothing but trouble right away.

The happiness my brother had carried was gone. The familiar look of his unwashed brown hair, sunken-in cheeks, and bloodshot eyes was enough to bring me to tears the instant I saw him.

I spent the next year begging him to leave her as I watched him wither away before my eyes. But he was in love. Whether it was with her or the high, I will never know.

I can't look away. Taking in the way they've aged. The tired look marring their features that didn't exist before. Wondering if they still feel like Michael was their answered prayer or just more pain they never deserved.

I wonder if they find forgiveness in the woman standing alongside of me. The one that fed his addiction more than her own. The counselor in me is desperate to find understanding. To look at her the same way I have the hundreds of people that walk through my door struggling with addiction. The way I saw my brother as a victim of circumstance beyond his control.

It seems damn near impossible as I watch the last of my family sink beneath the earth. I can't help but blame her for all of it.

Right now, she stands to my right, only feet separating us. Her black dress hanging loosely over her thin frame, highlighting the weight she has lost since I saw her last month. Her matted red hair thrown into a sloppy bun on top of her head, pieces falling out around her pale sunk in cheekbones, and dull gray eyes.

A soft laugh falls from her lips at something her friend says. To everyone else here it went unheard, but it shoots white fiery rage through my entire body. Anger begging me to set it free, begging me to defend my brother one last time from these people that swore they were his friends.

My nails dig into my palm, the pain enough to bring me back to standing here without causing a scene.

Can't you all see she killed him? My mind screams at all the sorrow filled faces surrounding us. I know they can't, though. In their eyes, my brother was no more than a relapsed addict desperate to escape it all.

I swallow down the bile climbing up my throat and glance over at the pastor again, praying he is about to wrap it up. I'm not sure how much more I can take. He shoots me a sad smile as he continues to talk. I scold myself for ignoring every word he is saying, but the noise in my head is deafening.

"You okay?" Trish leans in and whispers.

I try to reply, but the words are trapped in my throat. Her eyes shoot to mine as she wraps her arm tightly around my waist.

I simply nod my head yes even though every piece of me is screaming no.

The truth is, Trish is the only reason I haven't ended up with the same fate as my little brother. We both struggled when we first went into foster care after our grandmother's death.

Our foster family constantly reminded us how lucky we were that they took us both in. Any wrong move they'd happily send us back and we would find nowhere to go since we were both old. It could have been worse. We always had food and hot showers. They bought us nice clothes and gave us our own bedrooms, but aside from that, they treated us as if we didn't exist.

We had to ask permission to speak. Most times, they denied us. After months of being screamed at for saying even the simplest of words, I completely stopped talking all together. I woke up, did my countless chores, then locked myself in my room every chance I got. Michael, on the other hand craved interaction. He would sneak out every night, finding anyone willing to hang out with him. The people hanging out in the middle of the night were more than willing to share their demons with a lonely foster kid.

I hadn't spoken a word in over a year before I met Trish. She was the new girl in our eighth-grade class who everyone loved in no time at all. One day she was talking to a group of kids as they all looked at me and laughed, but not Trish. She walked right up to me and would not stop asking me questions. When I wouldn't answer, she would reply for me and move on.

She concluded my favorite food was pizza. I loved the color purple and played the piano. None of which were even close to correct. Finally, after a week, I couldn't take it any longer. I blurted out my favorite color was yellow and we have been inseparable ever since.

The pastor closes the prayer. Looking up, he locks eyes on me. I whisper a quick thank you. Before he says anything; I walk away. I know I should stay and thank those who showed up. But another second of listening to the people that swore they were his friends whisper among themselves is more than I can bear.

Their low snickers surround me. Swallowing down the lump in my throat, I pick up my pace. The sooner I get away from this town, the better. I lock-in on my beat-up Honda crammed to the roof almost comically with everything Trish and I own.

All I have to do is make it to my car and I can

leave this town and all the haunting memories tangled deep within it.

"Did you hear how he died?" Their careless words come from behind me like a bullet piercing through my back.

My steps falter, causing my knees to buckle beneath me. The cold dew from the grass soaking through these damn stockings. They are too tight, everything is too tight. I feel as though the breath is being sucked from my lungs. I desperately grasp at the high neckline of my dress, pulling it from my throat, which does nothing as I desperately suck for oxygen.

I know how he died, the memory of him lying awkwardly on the floor by his bed. The cold feel of his gray skin still seared into my fingers. The emptiness in his brown eyes that stared lifelessly at the ceiling. The denial. The CPR. *Thirty pumps. Two breaths. Thirty pumps. Two breaths.* The burning in my arms screaming at me to give up. The officer wrapping his arms around my waist, pulling me away as I fought with everything I had to get back. Me begging that officer to let me save my brother, and him telling me over and over it was too late. *The sirens. The screams. My screams. they won't shut off!*

"Damn it, Michael, why did you have to leave me?" The words fall from my lips, maybe as a whisper, maybe a scream. Not even I'm sure of my actions anymore.

Warm hands grab my face, breaking the fog that has wrapped through my brain. Trish sits on the wet grass in front of me. Bleach blonde strands of hair falling from her up-do into her face. Her bright blue eyes etched with worry are enough to push me to pull it back together.

Forcing a smile, I rise from the ground, pulling her up with me.

"How are we going to burn these hideous tights if they are both soaking wet?" I choke out.

She laughs, but it's as fake as the smile I've pasted on my face.

Chapter Two

Claire

I drag the knife through the tape of the box in front of me. Taking a breath as I wrap my fingers around the edges of the stiff cardboard, using every ounce of my power to attempt to rip them open.

"Just do it," I scold myself. Frustration that such a simple task seems to be impossible.

"Claire, it's only been a month since his funeral. You don't have to go through all of this stuff yet. Hell, you could leave them boxes sealed forever if that's what you need to do," Trish says leaning against the door frame.

She looks as exhausted as I feel. She never complains about the late nights and early mornings spent unpacking, even though it shows in the dark circles under her eyes.

"All he wanted to do was stay in New York. The minute he was gone, I packed up every piece of him in boxes and shoved them in an empty room in the middle of nowhere, Colorado," I say, swallowing back the tears threatening to spill out. "He would have hated it here."

"This is where you need to be. You gave up taking this job for months so Michael could be back home. He told you to take it back then so he wouldn't be mad at you for taking it now. You're the best counselor I know, and you've worked so hard to get this position."

"Yeah, a counselor that couldn't even save her own brother," I say, dropping my head onto the box beneath me.

The reality of the imposter I feel like slaps me in the face. Something I've been trying to shove down for months. She walks over and sits in front of me.

"You can't put this on you. You gave every piece of yourself trying to save him. If your boss had any doubts, she wouldn't have offered you the center again," she says as she gently grabs the box from under me, carrying it over to the pile stacked neatly under the double window. "You know you won't be able to save everyone, but you sure as hell make a difference in people's lives. You can't deny that."

I look around the room again. The hardwood floors and white walls only broken up by what feels like an impossible number of boxes containing my brother's entire life. This room feels like a definition of hell. The thought of digging through every memory of his eating away at me.

"I thought if I had the moving company pack it all up, it would be easier to go through than seeing it all in its place in his room," I tell her as I choke back the panic climbing up my throat.

"It's been a hard month. You lost your brother, then packed up and moved from the only place you've ever known. Then the apartment fell through. We might have been sleeping in one of these boxes if your boss didn't add housing to the job for you," Trish says to me reaching out to help me off the ground before wrapping me tightly in her arms. "It could take a month, or it could take forever. No matter how long it takes, you need to stop being so hard on yourself. If anyone wouldn't want you to beat yourself up, it would be Michael. Remember what he always said?"

"Worrying is for people who want gray hair and wrinkles," I recite, a laugh breaking through the pain that has clouded most of my favorite memories of him.

"We have been unpacking for weeks. I think it's getting to us. I don't even know when I last washed my hair." She pauses, reaching up to the tangled blonde mess on top of her head and cringes. "Let's go out tonight. Clear our heads and get back at it tomorrow."

"Maybe you're right." I sigh. The weight of everything seems too heavy. "I need to get out of here. I'm losing my mind."

"There is a small bar about ten minutes away with live music Friday nights. We need showers. You need an outfit. It's already eight. We should probably head out soon," she says, her just exhausted voice now full of energy.

"I will be right there," I tell her, smiling at the burst of joy that finally found its way into the house.

She looks at me for a second, assessing if I am okay.

"Go." I laugh. "If I get there first, I am going to pick my outfit."

A horrified look crosses her face.

"Absolutely not. I'll meet you up there," she yells back at me, already halfway up the steps.

I turn back, taking one more look around the room before grabbing the cool metal handle and shutting the door, unsure of how long it will be before I open it again.

"What do you think the guys are like out here? You think they are cowboys? I could use a good cowboy," Trish says from the passenger seat, reapplying lip gloss in the mirror for the tenth time since we left the driveway five minutes ago.

"You?" I ask, with confusion in my tone. "What

about Brett?"

She freezes, something flashing across her face before plastering on a smile that is too large to be real.

"I broke up with him before we left," she states simply as if she didn't just drop a bomb that her six-year relationship had ended.

"I thought he was moving down here after he finished this last work project?"

"There is no work project." She shrugs.

"And you are okay with this?"

"Yup, it's better this way." Her voice clipped.

"Trish?"

"I said I'm good," she says, turning to me. "I just don't want to talk about it. It's been crazy. Can we just forget it and have a good night?"

"Yeah, sorry." I agree, nodding.

Silence takes over the car as I stare ahead. The only light on the street is my headlights. Finally, the endless fields surrounding us opens to the smallest town I have ever been to. A gas station sits on our left. The sign half lit up. Next to it sits the local market Trish and I visit once a week. The bricks are worn and cracked. The owners are an older couple that bicker at each other across the store while people shop. Honestly, they are the sweetest people I've met in my life. The supermarket back in New York would have been bigger than this entire town, but nothing in me misses the chaos of the city.

Across the street sits the bar. Every time we have been out this way, the building looked desolate. But tonight, neon lights glow across the front. The parking lot is filled with lifted trucks that flow into the neighboring field.

"Maybe this wasn't a great idea," I say, glancing over at Trish.

"Are you kidding? This looks amazing," she says. "This is the most human interaction I'm going to have for another month. We are going."

I shove back the anxiety, realizing she's right as I pull my car into the field, parking it in the first available spot before I talk myself out of it. Of course, it's sandwiched between two massive trucks, making me feel more out of place than ever.

Trish jumps from the car the second I shift into park. I follow behind, catching my reflection in the truck mirror by me. My make up darker than I would have ever dared to make it, but my blue eyes stand out more than normal. Soft sandy curls flow past my shoulders, reaching to the neckline of the black dress Trish forced me to wear.

"You are keeping that dress, by the way," Trish says as I turn to face her. The sadness wiped away completely and replaced with a huge smile.

"I'm not stealing your dress, Trish."

"Oh, yes, you are. Because I refuse to take it

back. That dress looked nothing like that on me. It was made for your curves," Trish says, looking at me with a reassuring smile. "I promise, you look amazing. Now, let's go have some fun before this humidity turns us into frizz balls."

She grabs my hand, dragging me behind her through the crowded bar doors, the cool air from the air conditioner welcoming us.

"Wow, it's packed here. Maybe I should try to find us a table while you order the drinks from the bar?" I say, craning my neck for a space over the crowd where we could sit.

"Good idea, Coke for you?" she asks, letting go of my hand and heading towards the bar. I nod and start my search.

The dance floor is to my left with people laughing and line dancing to a country song I've never heard before. A crowd has formed thickly around them, taking any table available.

I look back at Trish, eyes follow her as she walks through the crowd. In heels she towers above most of the other women at five-ten. I know most of the men in here are already thinking of ways to get the courage to approach her.

Back in New York, the modeling agencies practically threw themselves at her, begging her to work for them when they would see her on the street. She would just laugh in their faces and leave them standing there in shock when she denied them. Trish, built like a model with the brain of a genius, hides from almost everyone but me.

She walks up to the bar, squeezing in next to a man in a cowboy hat that towers over her. Not by accident, I'm sure. He looks over, a huge smile lighting up his face as he takes her in.

He should buy me some time to find us something.

I see a girl on the other side of the room grabbing her bag from the back of a chair. There is a chance it's a bathroom break, maybe just a trip up to the bar, but I am not risking losing the spot.

As I shuffle through the thick crowd, a deep laugh captures my attention. I turn and see the most beautiful man standing with a group of his friends. He seems to be ready to leave. His dark hair hangs across his forehead as he leans in and shakes one guy's hand. I scan down his fitted white t-shirt, just tight enough to make out the definition of his muscle's underneath.

Did I just drool? Claire, get a grip.

I rip my eyes up and lock onto a pair of piercing green ones staring back at me. A knowing smirk gracing his face.

Crap.

What's the best plan of action when you're caught staring down a man in public? Apparently, wave, because that is what I do. As my arm shoots up and my hand flies left to right, I internally curse myself.

Claire, you are an idiot that is going to die alone. My inner monologue screams at me, but it's too late to save myself. I continue to let my hand awkwardly fly through the air.

His one brow shoots up on his head and that's enough fuel to jerk my arm firmly back by my side, my eyes following suit and shooting quickly to the ground. The warmth of embarrassment climbs its way up my cheeks. Apparently, every rational thought of watching where I'm walking is thrown out the window, as my body collides with a hard chest. The five-inch heels Trish insisted I wear give way in slow motion. The unforgiving floor smashing into my tailbone, shooting pain up my spine. Which is quickly drowned out by the rain of freezing cold liquid cascading down my head. I run my hands down my now soaked face, trying to remove the burning alcohol which has seeped into my eyes.

Fantastic.

I have yet to look up, but I can feel the crowd gathered around me; the murmurs drowning out the music in the background. It feels like minutes drag by as I sit, attempting my plot to escape, when a pair of worn brown cowboy boots appear, almost touching my legs.

"Are you alright?" The deep voice that fills my ears asks.

I take the risk of looking up and locking eyes with the same green pair I was staring at only a few seconds ago.

That same gorgeous man is now leaning over top of me, reaching for my hand while I'm drenched in rum and coke.

Kill me now. Please, just take me from my misery. I beg God, as if he is going to just instantly grant my wish here and now. I will die alone. When I get home, I'll just buy the cat. First of many, I'm sure.

Realizing I am still staring at him. I reach out, grasping his hand, a small spark shooting through me as I allow him to hoist me to my feet.

My prayer obviously has fallen on deaf ears.

You know how they say everyone has the fight-or-flight response? Well, the fight in me must be dead because I currently feel like a trapped little mouse surrounded by a dozen starving cats.

I spot the glowing exit sign across the bar and without a word, not even a thank you to the sexy, green-eyed man, I walk away.

Let's be honest, I don't walk. I run, hitting shoulders all the way towards the door.

I shove through the crowd locked on the exit door, desperate to escape. When my hands hit the door, it gives way to the thick summer air; I embrace it, praying Trish somehow sees me run out.

The crowd outside of the bar quiets down as they take me in. I can only imagine how I look. I try my best to square my shoulders, focused on my car that now seems miles away. When I get there, I will text Trish to let her know I'm okay.

"Hey." It's the man from inside. I keep walking.

"Hey," he says again, running to catch up with me. "Are you okay?"

I stop, twisting around, causing him to almost barrel into me.

"Shit," he says, coming to an almost-instant halt. "Sorry to follow you out here. I just wanted to make sure you were okay."

"I'm fine," I state simply turning to walk the last few feet to my car, when I realize I gave Trish the keys to put in her bag.

I smack my hands on the door before collapsing against the side of it. The weight of it all is too much.

My brother is dead. Everything I try to do is a disaster. All I wanted was one night to forget it all and I can't even get that. I want to scream. Scream at how unfair life can be. Instead, I stare at the sky. Taking in the vastness of the stars unlike anything we had back at home.

"You sure you're okay?" The voice breaks through my silence and I look over to him standing awkwardly by the front of the car, looking unsure of if he should step any closer.

"Just trying to debate if I can afford to move

again," I say, trying to hide the break in my voice.

"Can I sit?" he asks, pointing to the ground next to me.

Stranger-danger screams in my mind, but I drown it out and pat the ground next to me as an invitation.

"If you want to join my pity party down here, sure," I tell him, refusing to look up. "I am sure whatever is going on inside is way more fun than this, though."

"I doubt that. They were driving me nuts. You gave me an excuse to leave," he says, sliding down next to me, following my gaze up to the endless stars.

"Thank you, for in there," I say, turning to face him.

When his eyes meet mine, I realize he is even more gorgeous up close. Sharp jaw peppered with dark hair, his eyes a bright green color that reminds me of the pieces of sea glass my grandfather and I would find on the beach when I was a child.

"It's okay, it's not every day a beautiful girl waves at me in a crowded bar. I feel honored." He laughs, causing me to blush. "I am just glad you're okay. It looked like you landed hard."

"Yeah, mostly just hurt my pride." And my tailbone, which was currently throbbing, but I figured I'd omit my butt pain to the hot stranger.

"So, you're new to town?" he asks.

"Yup, just out here making great first impressions." I say. "My best friend and I moved here last month. Figure we could use a break from unpacking."

"You realize if you move, you will miss out on this view, right?" I follow his gaze back up to the sky.

"Well, it looks like I am staying then because this view is the most amazing thing I have ever seen," I say to him.

"It was for me too, before tonight," he says, eyes locked in on me. I scrunch my eyebrows in confusion, but he doesn't address it, just turns back to the sky, rubbing his jaw, seeming deep in thought as silence once again fills the air. "You know, they say coke makes a great fabric softener if you are worried about the dress."

I am not sure if he's being serious or trying to break the tension that has fallen around us, but a laugh falls from my lips. I think it is the first time in over a year and before I know it, tears are falling down my cheeks.

"I am so sorry," I say between breaths as I try desperately to pull myself together.

All the emotions I have held in for so long seem to pour out of me. Every tear I have swallowed back down from laughter, anger, sadness seems unending through the fit of giggles.

I look over at him, expecting a look of

annoyance. Maybe him running back to the safety of the bar. Instead, he stares at me with a huge smile.

"Sorry," I repeat the laughter, slowly dying out. "I can't remember the last time I laughed like that."

"You don't have to be sorry," he says, leaning forward gently, pulling a piece of hair that is now stuck to my cheek in the sticky coke.

We both freeze, eyes locked in on each other. Two complete strangers surrounded only by the light of the night sky. Thoughts pinball through my mind as his gaze drops to my lips, sending my heart into a frenzy. A man whose name I don't even know, but for the first time in my life, I don't care. I want to jump, consequences be damned.

I lean in slightly as he follows, pausing when the whisper of his breath brushes against my lips. A chance for me to change my mind if I want to when I hear Trish's voice break through the silence.

I jolt backwards. Every choice I've made up to this point hitting me full force.

"Claire Elizabeth Andrews!" she shouts as she scans around the bar, locking on me in an instant and running my way. I jump up to meet her as she reaches me, feeling him climbing to his feet behind me. "I am so sorry. I deserve an award for being the worst friend in the world. How did I miss that whole situation back there?" she blurts out in a rush, pausing when her eyes bounce to the stranger at my back.

"Ya know what? I can go back in. It seems you are being well taken care of out here. So sorry I interrupted." She quickly begins her escape, winking at me, without even trying to hide her attempt to shove me down this man's throat, hoping he devours me.

"Actually, I think I am ready to go if that is alright with you? I am sticky and gross, plus I have to figure out where I can buy a cat around here." She pauses, disappointment flashing through her face. She knows firsthand how long it has been since I have given a man the time of day.

"Are you sure?" she questions, and I nod in response.

"Yes," I pause. "Um… I'm sorry, I didn't catch your name."

"Tyler," he says, "It was nice to meet you."

"It's nice to meet you too, Tyler," she says, giving an overly obvious thumbs up. "I'm Claire's best friend Trish."

"On that note, it's definitely time to go." I laugh, trying to hide how absolutely mortified I am at myself right now.

"Tyler, thanks so much again for helping me out. Have a good night."

I climb into the driver's seat, watching as he

slowly walks away.

"What was that?" She laughs. "I know you're all anti-one-night stands, but he was worth breaking your rule. He was fine." I glance back even though I know I shouldn't, catching him looking back, and a smile cracks across his face.

I smile back, wishing I had let Trish walk away.

Chapter Three

Tyler

"Tyler, there is no way the guys can keep going today," Layton says, chucking the pail across the ground.

"I don't give a shit. We have to get these cows out of the sun before they give birth," I tell him as I pull my shirt up, wiping the sweat off of my face.

"The heat wave has been brutal this week. The guys are all beat. Someone going to have a goddamn heatstroke if you keep them out here any longer," he says I can see he's close to losing it himself. His sun-tanned face covered with streaks of mud and his shirt soaked through with sweat. "Listen, you know I am the last to complain. I know how far behind we are, but we are going to fall even further behind if we don't let the guys have a break."

"I know," I say, defeated, dragging my hand through my hair. "I just can't risk losing any more cows this year."

"I'll send all the guys home for the rest of the day and we can start fresh tomorrow," he says, putting a hand on my shoulder. "We will get them all there, I promise. I just went and checked them all. Not a single cow is in distress. We can't risk our guys though, it's not right."

"Yeah," I say to him. I know he's right, but nothing stresses me out like my animals not being safe. "Text the guys. Tell them to call it a day."

I walk toward the house before I hear him agree. The second the ranch empties, I get back to work until the sky is so dark, I can't even see in front of me. Exhaustion doesn't even touch the tiredness I feel. Every ounce of my body aches. I know I should take a break too, but every time I feel like I can't push any further; I picture my dad, the work he put in to build this place. He trusted me enough to run it, having no clue where I was headed. At least he died before he was disappointed, I think to myself.

The morning starts early, my body protesting as I pull myself from sleep before the sun comes up.

My muscles scream at the hell I've been putting them through. I know Layton would lose it if he knew all the extra hours I was pulling.

Part of me feels bad for lying. I have been on edge all week, snapping at the simplest things. The guys have all been tiptoeing around me. I know they don't deserve it, but the lack of sleep is eating away at me.

The smell of coffee hits me as I walk towards the kitchen. Luke sits in his wheelchair by the stove frying up eggs.

"When did you go to bed?" he asks, not bothering to look over his shoulder.

"I don't even know," I admit before collapsing on the island, laying my head against the cool granite.

"You need to take a break," he says, placing a thermos of coffee in front of me.

"I'll take a break when all the work's done," I tell him, dragging myself from the chair, coffee in hand. "I'll be back."

He just watches me leave. I can't tell if the look on his face is worry or disappointment.

I jump in my truck, taking a long sip from my cup, knowing all the coffee in the world won't be enough to wake me up.

The roads are empty. Most people in this town are filling the pews of the church I'm passing. Maybe I should be next to them all. Singing songs out of their old worn hymnals. Just walk in like I haven't been missing from my spot for the last twelve years.

Sundays now mean I don't have to deal with other people when I shop this morning.

My mom has been begging me to go with her for years. The last time I sat in those worn pews was a few months after the accident. The whole service, my skin crawled with the sensation I no longer belonged. A thick black sludge coursing through me with a hate I didn't recognize towards no one but myself. When the service ended, I calmly walked through the solid wooden doors, accepting the man I used to be was dead and the man I'd become no longer deserved grace.

I know my mom is in that church right now. Still saving me a spot next to her. The day I walked out of that church was the last time I saw her. I try to convince myself that it's protecting her. That she doesn't need to see the truth of who I've become. Resent and anger are the only things that course through my soul. In reality, I can't bear seeing her pain again. Pain I know I have caused.

Who knows, maybe God is really as forgiving as they say he is. I just wish I could fathom an ounce of forgiveness for myself.

I'm almost to the store when I see a silver car pulled to the side of the road with a small woman kicking the tire repeatedly. I am still too far to make out who she is, but I am thanking God I'm not that tire right now. As I get closer, I see her blonde hair pulled up into a ponytail as she turns towards the sound of my truck. I know she can't see me yet, but the breath rushes from my lungs.

I pull up slowly behind her, taking in the car's shape. It is an old Honda rust lining the bottom bumper.

Jumping out of my truck, I walk up to her as she kicks the tire one more time. Not to my surprise, her kick doesn't magically cure whatever is wrong, but it draws my attention to the massive black puddle under her feet.

A look of shock passes over her face as she looks up at me. Her hair plastered to her forehead from the summer heat. Before she looks up at the sky. I follow her gaze but see nothing. "Just trying to see if you have a call light like Superman or not."

"Nope, no call light, and I think you mean Batman," I laugh.

"What?" She looks at me like I've grown a second head.

"Batman had a call light... the Bat Signal." She continues to stare at me, eyebrows scrunched in confusion. "Anyway... what happened?"

"I don't know. Everything was fine. Then something started banging. I slowed down, but there was a big bang. By the time I got it to the side of the road, it died." I can't help the cringe that passes my face because I know there is a good chance her car can't be saved.

"Please don't tell me it's something bad. I only need this car to last me one more month until I get my bonus from work."

"I can tell you it's not bad, but I honestly think I'd be lying to ya if I did."

"Crap, crap, crap," she whispers, pacing back and forth.

"Let me call you a tow. I can give you a ride."

She huffs out a small breath, ready to argue, but I point to the phone already against my ear and she walks over to her car. My gaze travels down the curves of her body as she walks away before I feel like a complete creep and turn, leaning against the tailgate of my truck. She walks back into my view with a purse in one arm and a cat carrier in the other.

"You really don't have to do this. I can find someone to come pick me up." She looks down, kicking a small rock with her shoe.

"Well, it seems pretty silly to make someone go out of their way when I'm right here." I pause for a second, remembering this girl doesn't know me at all.

"Unless you don't feel comfortable with me driving you, then by all means, call someone."

"No, it's not that. I just feel bad for making you drive me home," she says. Apparently accepting defeat and walking to the passenger side of the truck, opening it before I have the chance to get it for her.

I hop in the driver's side of my beat-up Ford. "So, where are we going?"

"My house is up on Oldsmill," she says, pointing the opposite way her car is facing.

"Is that where you were heading when you broke down?" I ask, glancing at the empty carrier sitting on her lap.

"No," she whispers.

"Well, where were you going?"

A blush creeps up her neck, the same one she had the other night sitting there, sticky with coke making my mind go all kinds of places it shouldn't.

"You're going to judge me."

"I promise I won't," I reply.

"I was going to the animal shelter to adopt a cat," she says, glancing over at me.

"Why would I judge you for that?"

"I live that way," she says, pointing behind us.

"I know, but your future cat currently lives this way," I tell her, looking down at my watch. "And considering it's Sunday, the shelter closes in about an hour."

She stares in the rears view as we pull away, watching her car fade in the distance.

"Thank you," she says softly, twisting her hands in her lap as she looks over at me.

"Glad I can help." I say, taking a second to really look at her.

I knew she was gorgeous last night under the lights as she waved at me across the bar, but sitting here next to me, I can see just how beautiful she really is.

I must stare a second too long because her cheeks flush and she turns away. I turn my attention back to the road. We were only a few minutes from the shelter, so it doesn't take long before I've parked and we're walking inside.

"Welcome to Pets Haven," the lady at the front desk greets us as we walk in. "Were you interested in looking at our adoptable animals today?"

"I was hoping to see the cats you have," Claire states, a warm smile lighting up her face.

"Oh yes, we have so many cats right now. I am sure you will find one," she says as she walks from behind the desk. "Follow me this way."

I can practically feel the excitement buzzing off of Claire as the woman leads us towards a door, the sound of meows reaching through it.

"This here is our kitten's corner. There are lots of choices in here three months and younger." She turns looking at Claire and I.

"I was actually hoping to adopt an adult cat. I figure these little guys have a much easier time finding a home than those do," Claire tells the woman.

The worker skips to the next door, ushering us

inside the room with a huge smile. "Here are our adult cats. Every cage is full, so take your time."

Small cages line the walls with furry creatures rubbing against the sides, meowing. She starts at the beginning, taking in each cat, stopping at a couple to read their information.

I do not know what to do. I don't do well with small animals. Give me a horse. I am in my glory. Cats are not really my thing. I reach my hand towards the cage of a fluffy orange cat. The paper says his name is Cheeto. He reminds me of Garfield. I swear he gives me a dirty look before he hisses and swats at my outreached fingers.

"So, anything catching your eye?" I ask as I watch her read the paper of a white cat.

"I thought I would instantly know which cat to pick, but they are all so cute that it's hard to choose." She sighs, still walking along the wall of cages.

Before I can get out a word, a woman comes in, a small carrier in her hands, and a scowl etched into her brow. She looks up at us and gives us a sad smile before walking past Claire to a cage toward the end of the row. I want to believe she is about to take whatever cat is in that cage to its new family, where it can live happily ever after, but the look on her face says otherwise. Claire must catch on as well, because she is instantly over to the woman's side.

"Did someone get a home?" Claire asks hopefully.

The woman looks up at her and gives her a flat smile.

"Unfortunately, no. Charlie here is our longest resident. He has been here almost three years. Being here is getting harder and harder on him and with the new intakes, we just don't have enough space," she replies with a sigh.

"I will take him!" Claire says before she even looks into the cage.

Warmth shoots through me. A foreign feeling I try to shove away as I watch her excitedly walk to meet the cat she just declared hers.

The worker's face lights up. Part of me wonders if this was part of the plan to get poor Charlie a home, but props to them because it worked. Claire steps to look into the cage, smiling big at her new friend, and I follow behind.

As soon as my eyes hit the creature pinned to the back corner of the cage, I look at the worker. She gives me a look that says she knows every thought running through my head and pleads with me to silence them.

Charlie is almost completely bald, aside from a few random patches of black fur that poke out haphazardly across his body. His eyes take up most of his face in a look of pure terror and he is skin and bones. It has got to be the ugliest cat I have ever seen. Yet Claire is looking at him like he is the cutest thing she has ever laid eyes on. Part of me hates Charlie right now.

It hits me I'm jealous of a cat and I have never been more disappointed in myself.

"He's the one!" she declares without question. She looks back at me, her entire face lit up with excitement that she has apparently found her dream cat. I instantly wipe the panicked look from my face and smile back, an actual smile because God, this girl is something else.

"Oh, that is great news!" the worker says, letting out a breath I am pretty sure she was holding. "I will go get the paperwork ready for you," she says as she rushes from the room before Claire can change her mind.

"Isn't he perfect?" she gushes. "I mean, I know he isn't as fluffy as the rest of the cats, but maybe with some love, his hair could grow back. But if not, he has just got to be the cutest thing I have ever seen."

"I think if anyone can make it happen, it will be you," I say, shooting her an amused but reassuring smile.

"Thank you so much, Tyler, for bringing me here. You saved Charlie. Just imagine if I didn't make it in time." She turns and wraps her arms around me, pinning me into an enormous bear hug.

At first, I tense, but then allow myself to relax into her. God, she feels good wrapped in my arms, her head hitting right at my chest.

"Here it is!" the worker exclaims.

Claire jumps away from me, scribbling her name across the documents as the worker fights Charlie into the tight carrier behind us.

"Oh, buddy, I am so sorry. I promise you are going home. I'm going to take care of you and you will never be alone again," she coos to the stressed cat over her shoulder.

I know at that moment I need to stay away. Save all the good inside of her from the darkness burning through me, ready to destroy.

"Hey." She breaks me from my fog. "Are you ready to go?"

I look down to see Charlie safely tucked into his small gray carrier. His bony frame shoved into the back of the plastic carrier; his eyes somehow even wider than they were a few minutes ago.

"Yup, let's get this guy to his new home." I say, letting the smile easily light my face as I tell myself over and over, this is the last time I let myself close to her.

Chapter Four

Claire

I rush into the house before Tyler has even left the driveway. Climbing the worn porch steps two at a time as my heart beats wildly. I feel like a teenager again as I slam my back into the door, sliding down it. My cheeks heated and my mind racing with how can someone so easily make me feel things I am not sure I ever have before.

"Why do you look so disheveled?" I jump at the sound of Trish's voice.

She's sitting across the room on the couch, her eyebrows almost touching her hairline as she takes me in.

"I—" I pause, unsure of what to even do. "This is Charlie," I say, opening the door to set our new friend free, hoping he is a good distraction from the show I just put on unknowingly. He sits frozen for half a second before darting out of the carrier. Trish quickly pulls her feet up wrapping her arms around them.

"Is that a cat?" she asks, looking slightly horrified at the creature I've released on our living room floor.

"Yes, be nice. He is going to help us with our mouse problem," I say, hoping to earn our new friend some brownie points.

"That's if he comes out from under the couch ever again," Trish says, horror still etched into her features. "What's wrong with him?"

"What do you mean, there is nothing wrong with him?"

"It looks like you just set Gollum free in our living room. Is he friendly at least?"

I shush her, not wanting our new friend to hear her cruel words. She just shakes her head, staring at the couch like she's mildly afraid he will burst out and attack her.

"Just give him time. He has had a tough life and needs to learn to trust us." I grab two small bowls, filling them with cat food and water, hoping to lure him from his hiding spot. After shaking the bowl a few times, I admit defeat by placing it on the floor next to the water and falling onto the couch next to Trish.

"Okay, well…" she says, finally looking over at me. "Do I start at the fact that our car is missing or that you have that same look on your face you did when Mark Reeves held your hand on our eighth-grade field trip?" Trish asks.

"Listen, holding hands with Mark was the peak of my eighth-grade year," I say, dropping my eyes to my feet. "And the car may be dead,"

"Dead? What do you mean, dead?" she asks, jumping to her feet throwing the front door open to check the driveway as if she is being punked.

"Like undrivable and unfixable, dead." I cringe, the gravity of the situation hitting me at once.

Tyler made it so easy not to panic about the fact that I literally had no car to get to work, or anywhere else, for that matter. Trish, thankfully, switched to working from home after the move. But tomorrow is my first day in my very own drug and alcohol center as a counselor. A position I worked so hard to earn.

My boss said she had been wanting to offer the position to me for months, but knew I wouldn't be able to leave Michael behind. I asked her if she still felt I could handle the position since I couldn't even save my own brother. She told me my job isn't to play God. I won't be able to save everyone, but she had client after client come to her and tell her how much I had made them feel like a person again. Words that Trish constantly reminds me, no matter how much they feel like a lie. I knew how amazing this opportunity was, and I would be a fool to turn it down.

"What are you going to do about work in the

morning?" Trish asks. I can tell she's just as worried about our situation as I am. This isn't like New York, where we could walk to just about anything in ten minutes. Still, I knew my job wasn't too far from the house. I had driven there throughout the last few weeks, getting everything ready, and it had only taken about ten minutes.

I pull the address my boss had sent me up on my phone's navigation.

"It's only seven miles away. I can do that. I ran track in high school. How hard can it be to walk?"

"High school was almost ten years ago. I'm not sure it's going to be that easy," she states like I am crazy.

"Seriously, I will be fine. Just until I get my first couple of checks, and we can get the car fixed or buy something new."

"I will chip in, too. I used the car just as much as you. I still feel like this is a terrible idea. Claire, seven miles is far. What if there are bears, or worse, people?" She shivers at the thought.

"I will bring my pepper spray and my phone. If anything happens, I will call you," I tell her as I walk towards my room.

"Good luck calling me if you're being eaten by a bear!" she yells down the hallway.

I laugh, but quickly I search *what to do if a bear attacks you* on my phone. Apparently, they make bear spray. I look down at the small, bedazzled pepper spray resting in my hand and cringe. I'm sure it's close enough for now, I try to convince myself before climbing into bed, sleep claiming almost instantly.

The gravel crunching in the driveway shoots a familiar dread through my body. I don't need to look out the window to know who pulled in. I rush to my six-year-old brother, Michael's, room before I can even process it, but this routine is engraved in my mind.

Twisting open the handle on the door, I am greeted by him, playing with his trucks on the rug. His mousy brown hair stuck up chaotically across his head. He glances up at me and the smile that was gracing his tiny face falls. His favorite toys, thrown to the ground before running to my side.

Taking his hand, I use everything in my power not to let the fear masking his innocent brown eyes break me.

I bring myself back to the moment, getting us to the safety of my bedroom. I twist the lock behind me, walk across the room, and pull him into my chest before sliding down the wall. The silence that clings to the world around us almost seems serene. There is finally a sense of peace in our home, but I know what follows this peace is nothing less than Hell on Earth.

Michael trembles beside me. "Michael, it's going to be alright, I promise I will protect you." My voice comes out confident and strong. Inside, though, I am anything but.

The door smashes against the wall in the living room, causing both Michael and I to wince. I tighten my grasp around his waist as he buries his head deeper into my chest. His light brown strands tickling my chin.

"Where are you, you whore?" Our dad's slurred words fill my ear, the hatred lacing them so strong goosebumps break along my skin. Mama swears there was a time when he didn't speak like this, but I sure don't remember it. "I know you are here. Your car is in the driveway." His words break through the silence once again.

"Stop screaming, Frank. The kids can hear you." Mama always tries to keep her voice steady. She swears she can save him from the evil that lies beneath his skin.

"You think I give a shit what those kids hear?" Venom laces dad's words as he spits them at her. I throw my hands over Michael's ears, trying my best to save him from their hate.

He is drunk again. Our dad is drunk more than he isn't anymore. I told my mama she should call the police when things get like this. I am tired of watching the tears stream down her bruised cheeks after it's over.

Every time I say to call the police, she goes into a fit, saying he works so hard to change. That if I ever call the police, I will never see her or Michael again. I can't imagine my life without them both. So, I sit almost every day locked in my room, Michael wrapped in my arms, with nothing but a wall protecting us from the devil himself.

"Where are they, Anna? You hidin' my kids from me? You think they shouldn't see their daddy like this?" *Dad doesn't normally pay us any mind. The days he does, though, are always the worst.*

My mom got postpartum after we were born. She became a shell of the woman she once was, according to our dad. Now we have to pay for ruining his once perfect life.

The sound of glass crashing into the wall outside my room causes me to jump once more. All I can do is pray that my hands clamped to Michael's ears are doing their job.

"Leave them alone, Frank. They are our children. They have done nothing wrong!" *Her voice is loud and confident, something I know he hates.*

I brace myself. The sound of his hand across her face fills my ears, causing the already large knot in my stomach to grow. You would think after years of this, the sound wouldn't phase me like it still does.

Most days it's a hit or two, then comes the pathetic sobs before he goes to sleep it off. Then the next night he comes home and does it over again. This time, the sound doesn't stop. The sounds of slaps morph into loud thuds, and my mom's screams become hauntingly low. I run to the phone as silent as my feet will carry me and dial nine one one.

"Please help!" comes out in a strangled sound from my throat, tears sting at the backs of my eyes, desperate to be set free. "My dad is hurting my mama. Please hurry!"

I don't realize how loud I am until I hear my dad screaming at the door. The hate in his voice is unlike anything I have ever heard, shooting an ice-cold shiver down my spine. I toss the phone and hurl my body against the door, hoping that will do something, anything.

"You little shit! I'm going to kill you and your brother! Both of you are no good little bastards," Dad shouts.

His steel-toed boots thud against the wood of the door, causing pain to burst through my side. I freeze. He is going to kill us, and we have nowhere to hide.

"This is your fault. You destroyed her." Each word he says slices deeper into my chest as splinters of wood soar past me. "She was fine until you were born."

I look down at Michael's tiny features. First, I

take in his brown hair that is so filled with cowlicks it never lays flat no matter what mama tries. Then his beautiful light brown eyes that are slightly large for his face and have always reminded me of a shiny new penny. I lock every detail of him deep inside of me and then I pray.

"God, you can take me away from this world if you've gotta, but please protect Michael. Let him finally be safe and free. Let him finally get to be a kid. I will do anything if you can save him."

Smiling at Michael, a strange peace blankets over me. This is the end of the pain.

The wood cracks and splits. My body becomes numb to the sharp thuds against my ribs. I embrace it and step back, shoving Michael in the closet before grabbing a lamp from my nightstand. I brace myself between the splintered door and the closet. I know I can't win this fight. I've seen mama lose time and time again, but I will give it everything I can to keep him from getting into that closet.

A hole rips through the door in front of me. I stand my ground, the silver base of my bedside lamp digging into my skin, causing a warm trail of blood to drip down my wrist. His hand reaches through the jagged hole, fumbling for the lock.

Oddly, the fear that consumed me a few minutes before has vanished. In its place is nothing but searing rage. Rage that he's hurt mama again. I am sure she will be at the hospital this time, since she'd never let him get to us. Anger that at thirteen years old, I cannot be a kid like all of my friends. More than anything though, anger for the little boy smothering his fear in my sweatshirt in the closet. The little boy who deserves so much more than this life my dad has given him.

His hand hits the bottom of the knob, twisting to fumble the lock when the sound of sirens wail through the room.

I shoot up from my bed. The sound that was once sirens morphs into the steady beeping of my alarm clock shrieking through my room. I grab my phone from my table. Five A.M. Throwing on my outfit, I toss my work shoes into my bag and head out the door. I don't have to be at work until eight, but I want to be sure I am not late, and I honestly wasn't sure how long it would take me to walk seven miles.

It doesn't take long for me to regret my decision. The roads here are dark, with no streetlights lining them. Every so often I hear rustling coming from the woods along the road, and I think for sure I am about to be a bear's breakfast. I glance at my phone's clock. One hour in. I must be getting closer now. I think as the road lights up from behind me. There hasn't been a single car in the last hour. I pick up my pace, attempting to outrun the approaching vehicle, thanking Trish for the extra dose of paranoia this morning. The engine grows louder as it comes up on my back, slowly passing around me before the red of the brakes light up the street and it pulls over directly in front of me.

Fear grips me. Bears were far from the worst case; I think to myself as every worst-case scenario runs through my head. The door swings open, the interior light casting a shadow on the tall, muscular man stepping out. He is only feet away. There is no way I can outrun him. Maybe if I catch him by surprise, it will help my chance.

I run towards him, clutching my pepper spray tightly and pressing down on the button. I scream, praying for someone to hear me.

Nothing, the button doesn't budge. I slam my finger down again, now reeling backwards away from the fate I am sure I just sealed for myself.

"It's me!" the man yells, ducking my unsuccessful attempt to defend myself. Tyler's voice instantly registering.

"Holy crap, you scared me!" I yell at him, clutching my chest to slow my heart rate, afraid it may beat right out of my chest.

"I see that. I'm sorry I just saw you walking and realized you might not have a way around with your car being broken down, so I wanted to make sure you were okay," he says.

"I'm okay." I glance at my GPS and realize it is taking me way longer to walk than I had planned. "I only have four miles to go, I say, faking a smile.

"Jump in. I'll drive you," he says, walking to the passenger side of his truck.

"Tyler, you do not have to keep saving me. Literally every time we meet, you're rescuing me. I'm pretty sure that's not how this is supposed to work," I say, feeling bad for making him go out of his way again.

"I am sure New York wasn't like this, but out here, when you see someone needing help, you help them if you can. I have a perfectly good truck that can get you four miles a lot faster than you can walk it. Also, if I am being honest, the idea of you walking alone stresses me out. So, if you would like, you can walk, but I am going to follow you and make sure you get wherever you are going safely," he says, waiting for me to make my choice.

"Fine," I say as I walk around the truck, throwing my arms in the air dramatically before climbing into the passenger seat. "but only because you will look like a weirdo following me. Wouldn't want someone getting the wrong idea and call the cops or something." I try to look serious, but I can't help but grin. He doesn't even attempt to hide the victorious smile on his face as I collapse against the seat. The coolness from the truck's air conditioner wraps around me as I try to rub the cramps from the back of my legs.

"You, okay?"

"Yeah, I didn't realize how out of shape I have gotten, I guess." I laugh. "It's been a long time since I have walked like that.

"Well, it's going to be a long time again. I'm going to drive you to work until you get your vehicle situation figured out," he says matter-of-factly.

"Absolutely not," I argue back. "I am sure you have a lot more important things to do than drive some random woman you just met back and forth five days a week for who knows how long."

"I have nothing more important than making sure you don't get yourself killed walking to town every day," he states. "I know this is a nice town, but no one should walk alone, especially if they don't have to when their friend has a truck that drives."

We are still pulled to the side of the road. I have him locked in a stare.

"Is that what we are? Friends?" I challenge. "A woman you met a week ago that you know nothing about."

"How long do you have until you have to be at work?" he asks, blatantly ignoring me.

I look at my phone. "I have to be at work at eight, so about an hour."

He tosses his keys onto the dash. "Okay, so I know you hate bars, like bald cats, and moved from New York. Please tell me more about Claire Andrews."

I freeze, staring at him.

"I am not sure," I tell him truthfully. I don't even know if I know who I am.

"Okay, let's start easy. When is your birthday? What is your favorite color?"

"My favorite color is yellow, and my birthday is June twelfth," I answer. "What about you?"

"Favorite color is blue, and my birthday is February twentieth. What is your favorite food?" he continues.

"Chinese for sure. I love egg rolls," I tell him. "Let me guess, steak?"

"I do like a good steak. Where do you work? Do you like what you do? What is your family like? What are your hobbies?"

"I am starting today at New Hope Center on forty-eight. I am a drug and alcohol counselor, and on Monday mornings we have groups. I absolutely love what I do. I love to draw, and I had a little brother named Michael. He passed away right before we moved out here," I say, whispering the last part.

He looks at me with a sympathetic look that I hate. "I'm sorry."

I shoot him a soft smile. "It's okay," I reply. "But now you need to answer your questions."

"My brother and I own a ranch. We have almost fifty horses and over two-hundred cows with more to come. A couple of them are pregnant, and we have about a million chickens."

"Baby Cows!" I say excitedly.

"Yup, if you want to when they are born, I can bring you to the ranch to see them," he says with pride written all over his face.

"I would love that; I have never seen a real cow or horse." I tell him.

"Yeah, we can't have that. You are out in the country now. I think it's a requirement to at least see one cow," he tells me with a smirk.

"How about your hobbies and family?" I ask, trying not to overthink him making plans to see me again.

"I like to ride horses. My brother's name is Luke. He runs the business end of the ranch, and as if that isn't enough, he is in college to be a software developer. He definitely got the brains of the family. He's already created a ton but thinks a degree would help him go even further in the field," he says. "My mom lives in the town over in Alberta. My dad passed away when I was fifteen. He left the ranch to us."

"I'm sorry to hear that." A silence fills the truck as Tyler seems to disappear into his thoughts.

"I have always wondered what it would be like to ride a horse. I would never actually do it, though. They are too big," I say, trying to break through the moment.

"Oh, I will take that challenge to get you to ride at least once. It will change your life," He responds. I turn to face him, and we lock eyes.

"Now we aren't strangers. Does that make us friends?" he asks.

I pause. I have dated for months and never remotely felt this level of attraction, let alone just general comfort. Come to think of it, I don't think I have felt this at ease in my whole life. I think about the moment under the stars the day we met and my eyes travel to his lips, then back to his eyes that are now full of desire. The air in the truck seems to crackle beneath the intensity. My mind somehow racing and completely frozen with the thought of what's next when the sounds of my alarm blares through the silence, breaking the moment once again.

This time I can't deny it, though. He wanted to kiss me, and I would be damned if I didn't want it just as bad.

"I better get you to work. I wouldn't want you to be late on your first day," he says as he grabs the keys off the dash, shoving them in the ignition.

We sit in silence for the entire five-minute drive, my mind battling between how wrong it is that I am falling for a man I just met a few days ago. I mean, not that my track record is that great. I dated a guy for a year, only to find out that everything he told me was a lie. But even after a year, I felt nothing like what I feel when I'm with Tyler. Is it so wrong to want an attractive man after such a short period of time?

I realize Tyler has shifted the truck into park in front of the center. He is staring ahead, clenching his jaw as if maybe he's having the same internal struggle.

"Thank you so much for the ride, Tyler," I say, getting out of the truck to walk away when I hear his door swing open behind me.

"Wait," he yells after me.

I spin on my heels to face him.

"You didn't answer me. Are we friends now?" he asks.

"I am not sure," I say truthfully.

"Well, I'll need to keep working on it," he says. "What time do I need to be back to drive you home?"

I go to argue with him.

"Claire, if you don't tell me, I will just wait here all day. I've got nowhere to be."

"Fine, I get done at three," I reply, a giddy feeling flowing through me. "Thank you, Tyler."

His face breaks out in a grin before he climbs into his truck, waiting until I walk inside to drive away.

Chapter Five

Tyler

I lied to Claire. I am late as hell pulling into the ranch. As I turn the corner to park, I see the endless trucks parked in the field. Layton is leaning against the fence post waiting for me. He must notice the shock on my face because he smiles.

"Who are all these people?" I ask as I jump from the truck.

"Remember Levi?" He asks. "You helped him plow last year when he broke his leg. Chuck from down the street. You went and took care of their lawn for a year while he was overseas. Lenny from the corner store you bought him the security system after those kids kept breaking in and stealing."

I try to come up with anything to say, instead my eyes drift to the fields where at least a hundred people are out working.

"The guys went around after work last night asking if anyone could help out. It seems word spread around. I was just as shocked when I pulled in. It seems your tough guy act isn't working as good as you think since every single person who showed had some story you'd never told me about how you helped them." He laughs. "Every cow should be moved to the new field by tonight."

"How long has everyone been here?" I ask, grabbing the bags from the back of the truck. I feel like shit. I should have been here. All of these people working on my ranch. Helping me, and I wasn't even here. Guilt. Guilt that somehow I couldn't be in two places at once. Guilt that I feel like I once again let people down, even though there was no way for me to know. Endless fucking guilt.

"About an hour," he says following behind to help me unload the bags into the barn. "The question is, where were you? I have worked alongside you for ten years and not once have you been here after me."

"It was nothing," I tell him, throwing the bag down alongside the feed barrels.

He pauses, looking me up and down, the scowl on his face morphing into a shit-eating grin.

"I'll be damned," he says, walking away.

"What?" I demand, catching up to him.

"No, nothing," he says back. "I just would think that when my best friend met a woman, he would have told me about her is all."

"I did not meet a woman," I lie.

He stops so quickly in front of me, twisting around, I almost crash into his chest.

"Bullshit," he argues.

"I mean, I didn't, not really. There's a girl but —"

"I knew it!" he says triumphantly.

"It's not like that. I just met her last Friday night at the bar. I've seen her a couple of times since. Her car broke down, so I gave her a ride this morning and may have promised her rides back and forth to work for a while," I say, cringing as I realize how insane this is.

I am never late for work, nor do I ever leave early. I can't even remember the last time I gave a woman the time of day. My plate is full as hell. I go from work, then home to help Luke, and then back to work.

"I can hear you over thinking this, Tyler. Let yourself live a little. You obviously like this girl. I don't give a shit if it's only been a couple of days. I have never seen you act this way with anyone, ever." Layton butts through my thoughts, but it's too late.

I need to shut this down before it gets too far. I don't have time for a relationship, and a girl like Claire needs someone that is not me. *No one needs to deal with a man like me.*

"Let's just get to work. We have a lot to do," I tell him, anger lacing my words I don't mean to throw at him. He looks like he's about to argue, but I shoot him a look and he decides against it. "I need to go thank all these people who were nice enough to spend their day helping us."

"After that, head down to Lightning. Cole and Evan are working with him, but that horse is a nightmare, Tyler," he says. "He won't even let the guys get close to him. I know he was your grandfather's, but I think we may be in over our heads."

"Let's go down there first. I'll stop on and talk to people on the way," I reply, jumping on the Polaris.

As soon as we get close to the stables, the sound of a horse neighing fills the air. Cole and Evan stand by the fence, their shirts soaked through with sweat, watching the black beast run chaotically in circles.

Layton walks up to them as I stare at the mess on our hands. When my grandfather passed away a few months ago, he left Lightning to me with a note promising I wouldn't get rid of him. Nothing could have prepared me for the pain in the ass this horse would be.

"Boss, this horse is going to kill someone," Cole says, coming up alongside me.

"Let him tire himself out and then get him up for the day. We will try again tomorrow," I say, unwilling to go back on my word.

"Tyler, we have been doing this for over a month, and he is still just as insane," Evan complains.

"You heard what he said, Evan, do your damn job," Layton says, walking up to me. "That horse is a danger, Tyler, but I get it."

"I know," I say defeated, "What else do we have today?"

I ask, turning away from the chaos behind me like it doesn't exist.

"There are a couple cows in Pasture A that are due for their IBR shots. I figured we could get that done on the way to help move the rest of the herd," he says, jumping in the passenger side of the Polaris.

"So, this girl, is she hot?" he asks as I pull onto the dirt trail.

"Layton," I say calmly.

"Yeah?"

"Shut up."

"Thank you so much for everything. Let me know if you ever need anything," I say as the last of the helpers leave the field. Looking around at every cow, now safe in their new home.

"Can't beat this," he says, looking out with me.

"I am still trying to wrap my mind around this whole day." I say, still shocked at the number of people that came out and helped us.

"If it wasn't for you, I doubt it would have happened. You've built a great name for this place."

"Layton," I say, breaking his attention from in front of us. "You know where the old Mavis building is on forty-three?"

"Yeah?" he answers, a question in his tone.

"Cool, go there and pick up a girl named Claire. She is about this tall." I motion how tiny she is with my hands. "Blonde hair, blue eyes."

"Aren't you supposed to be picking her up?"

"I am going to head down and check on Lightning again. See how they made out?"

"You know how they made out. It's been the same every day for the last month."

"I'm just going to go down there."

"Tyler, don't do this. I won't ask about her again."

"Here, give her this," I tell him, tossing a new pepper spray his way. Shoving down the feeling I'm making a huge mistake. He looks at the spray in his hand looking up at me with question.

"Hers is broken."

"Tyler, come on." I don't respond. I just jump in

my truck.

"Don't you think a random, giant man coming to get her may freak her out?" he says, tossing his arms up in defeat.

I look at him. He is slightly intimidating at six-six, but he is nothing more than an enormous teddy bear.

"Just tell her I sent you, and I am sorry, but I got tied up." He looks at me and the field of cows that have all gotten their shots.

"Yeah, man, I will just tell her after we finished literally every task for the day, but you decided to be a bitch and not come," he bites out.

I just hang my head because I know he's right. I am a bitch.

"Sounds good. I'll see you later," I say as I drive off. I hear Layton yelling he's just kidding in the background, but I know he wasn't.

Five minutes later, I'm pulling up to my house, throwing the truck in park, and stomping inside. I'm completely exhausted as I throw my keys on the counter, and I look up to see Luke giving me a questioning look.

"Rough day, I take it?"

"Something like that," I say, shaking my head at how stupid I am for refusing to pick up Claire.

"You want to talk about it?" he asks. "Maybe you need a night out. You said you were going out Friday, but you were back in an hour. Go get drunk and have some fun."

"I can't do that, Luke. I wouldn't feel right leaving you here for that long, and what if something happens if I am drinking? I can't help you." This argument with him drives me nuts. He is constantly pushing me away when all I want to do is take care of him. That's what I am supposed to do; I'm the reason he is in the situation he is in.

"Tyler, you're thirty years old. One day, you're going to meet a girl and move on with your life. Start a family and maybe not be so damn miserable all the time. I am not your responsibility. I am a grown man who can do everything for myself, like everyone else. You treat me like I'm still a little kid and I'm not! I appreciate all that you've done for me, but I want to live my life too," he says, frustration lacing his tone.

My blood boils.

"Not my fault! Are you kidding me? At thirteen years old, you did nothing wrong. You were the perfect kid while I was out wreaking havoc on our mom. The only reason you were at that party was because of me, because I was too stupid to think about anyone but myself. Now, look at you! You're going to spend the rest of your life in that damned chair because of me! So yes, you are my responsibility. I will spend the rest of my life taking care of you, dammit!" I shout across the room, my body shaking from the anger coursing through it at no one but myself.

"No, you will not, because I'm tired of it. I want freedom. I want to go out and do what I want. I have enough money to live on my own. Soon, I am going to be leaving. You have no choice but to let me go! I'm a grown man."

His hurt look is a slap in the face. I know he's right; I know it's time I let him live on his own, but I'm scared, dammit. I already thought I lost him once. What if he leaves and something happens? I know he thinks he doesn't need any help, but what if he does and I am not there?

"Look, it's been a really long day. Can we just talk about this in the morning?" Tomorrow, I'll convince him he needs me.

He throws his hands in the air and starts wheeling away. "Whatever, but I'm not gonna change my mind. I have been thinking about this for a while now. It's time for us to live our own lives, and I will not keep dragging you down. You will always be my brother, but I will never let you blame yourself for what happened to me. You could be exactly like me, but you seem to forget that."

I turn to argue more, but he's already in his room, slamming the door.

Chapter Six

Claire

"Have a great day," I say as the therapy group makes their way out.

The last person to leave, a man named Phillip, stops in front of me. He is a large man, probably in his fifties. An army veteran who told us about his daughter having a baby recently and not allowing him to have any part of her life until he proves he can get clean. There is a sadness buried so deep in his eyes, it's hard not to see the hell he's lived.

"I just wanted to say how thankful I am that you are here. You have no clue how much we needed someone like you. The last person they had out here was so cruel and judgmental. I think that's why you had such a small group today. Word will get around, and you will have a full house before you know it. I can just tell you're different." He smiles, giving me a light pat on my shoulder, turning to leave before I can reply.

I close the door, twisting the lock before leaning against it as the weight of the day tries to pull me down. I have heard the stories before, but after losing Michael, they feel even stronger than they used to. Like I am finally seeing the hell through his eyes instead of through mine.

There were only five people here today. I hope what Phillip said is true, and soon everyone in this town that needs help will fill the seats in the room. I glance across at the big black and white clock. Tyler will be here in twenty minutes. I can't help the giddy feeling that takes over me as I tidy up the center for the night.

If today has reaffirmed anything, it is that life is short. Tyler most likely isn't my true love. I realize this, but I have spent so many years afraid of love because of my parents. So many wasted years hiding from what may be instead of trying. I have seen love in my life. My grandparents were the definition of love until the last breath. I'll be damned if I don't crave that.

The center is spotless in record time. Throwing open the door, I welcome the warmth of the summer air against my air-conditioned skin. I quickly lock up and plop down on the curb. Checking my phone to see it's already five minutes past three.

Maybe I'll just walk right up and kiss him. No, that may be too pushy. I will wait until it feels right, but this time I won't hesitate. *No more fear, Claire. It is time to let go and live.*

I look out at the empty parking lot surrounded by trees. The silence of the street making me second guess myself.

He just got hung up at work. Stop overreacting. He isn't even that late.

The sound of a truck pulling into the parking lot captures my attention and I jump up, feeling a smile pull across my face, only to realize it's not him. The lifted blue Chevy parks in the spot across from where I am sitting, a very tall man in a cowboy hat jumping from the driver's seat.

"I am sorry. The group has ended for the day," I say. "We meet again next Monday at ten, if you are interested in joining us."

"Actually, Tyler sent me to pick you up. My name's Layton. He got hung up at work and couldn't get here. He didn't want to leave you hanging, so he asked if I would come."

I hesitate for a second. Debating if I am once again going to jump into a random cowboy's truck, but the ache in my feet begs me to accept the invite.

I bite back the disappointment and shoot him a smile before walking to the passenger side of his truck. He runs over before I get to the door, opening it for me to climb in.

"Thank you for the ride," I mumble when he hops in the driver's seat. I should try to mask the disappointment in my tone, but it's too deep to hide.

"No problem," he says. "He asked me to give you this."

He hands me a black pepper spray. I stared at the sealed package in my hands.

"Is Tyler really stuck at work?" I ask, unsure if I want the answer.

He blows out a breath, focusing ahead, not saying a word.

"That's what I figured."

"If it makes you feel any better, Tyler is a good guy. He is just an idiot sometimes," he tells me, his words laced with the disappointment I feel.

"I'm guessing his promise to drive me back and forth isn't happening, either?" I ask, unsure if I want the answer.

He pauses, staring ahead for a second.

"If you want me to be honest with you, I don't know."

I nod and focus on the road.

"He seems really great," I mumble under my breath.

It hits me that Tyler must have given him my address when he pulls into the driveway. I jump out, yelling thanks before running into the house ready to wallow in self-pity over a man I have known for less than a week.

As soon as I open the door, Charlie shoots across the living room, flying back under the couch. I lean down, attempting to call him out, when a sound captures my attention.

I follow it to the bathroom where Trish is hunched over the toilet.

"Holy crap, are you okay?" I ask, grabbing a washcloth from the cabinet and wetting it with cool water before dropping beside her and placing it on the back of her neck, gathering her hair into my hand.

"I think I ate something that didn't agree with me for dinner last night. I have been so sick all day." She groans before leaning over the toilet again to throw up.

"Why didn't you call me?" I ask.

"Today was your first day. I didn't want to stress you out more than you already were," she answers before standing to go to the sink and wash her face.

"Let me grab you some new clothes. Throw those in a pile. I will wash them for you," I tell her as I run to her room, grabbing the first pair of pajamas I see and coming back.

I jerk to a stop outside of the open bathroom door. Trish is pulling her shirt over her head. Her back towards me, a long thick scar starts just under her right shoulder and drags down almost to her hip. I can't move. I am frozen in place, staring at the poorly healed line. She throws the shirt on the floor before looking up, catching me in the mirror. The horror etched on my face is undeniable.

"Trish, what happened?" My question comes out just above a whisper. She freezes, staring at my reflection, tears threatening to spill from her eyes.

"It is nothing. Just give me the clothes." Her voice clipped, but I don't move. She whips around, snatching the garments from my hands.

"That wasn't there," I say, desperately digging through memories of how she kept this hidden.

"Seriously, Claire, it's not a big deal. It happened a while ago," she says before slamming the bathroom door in my face. The sounds of her sobs break the silence that fills the house.

"Trish," I beg through the wooden door.

"Just leave me alone," she says through sniffles.

"I can help you. Please, just talk to me," I say softly.

Silence fills the air. I think she may just never come out when the door swings open.

"You can't help me, Claire. This is why I didn't tell you. I knew you would get all stressed out trying to fix it when you can't," she says, shoving past me.

"You're my best friend. Of course, I would try

to help you. What is wrong with trying to help someone you love?"

She stops at the door to her room, annoyance all over her face.

"I watched you with Michael, Claire. You forgot to eat, you didn't sleep, for the love of God, when is the last time you got laid?" she pauses, waiting for my reply, but I honestly don't know. It's been years. "My point exactly. You constantly think you can save everyone, but you can't. I refuse to be the reason you bury yourself again."

The door slams in my face, leaving me with no other choice but to walk to my room. The splintered pieces of my past, threatening to rip apart into a thousand tiny shards. My heart is begging me to turn around and fight for the truth, but my mind tells me to give her time.

I know that look all too well. One I never thought I would see on someone as strong as Trish. The look that says someone has broken you. I drop to my bed, staring at the ceiling, playing back all the moments over the last year in my head.

The time she called me from her trip to Hawaii with Brett and said they decided to stay two more weeks stands out. She had a work project due and had been stressed about even taking a week off. She sounded so happy over the phone, though I was glad she had decided to take the extra time off.

When she got back, she was constantly wincing in pain. When I asked her what happened, she said she had gotten a horrible sunburn on her back. That shut down all of my concerns, and I let it go. Maybe if I hadn't been so distracted, I would have seen the signs that she was hiding something.

I was so caught up in Michael's addiction, I missed it. My best friend had suffered alone while I was desperately trying to hang on to any pieces I had left of my brother.

I bring my pillow over my head, screaming into it before tossing it at the wall. It does nothing to drown out the rage boiling inside of me. I want to jump in my car and drive all the way back to New York. I want him to suffer for hurting her, but I know it's impossible.

"Michael, what the hell am I supposed to do?" I ask the dark ceiling, praying an answer magically appears. "If you were here, I could go right to you. You would talk me through it. You'd probably already be in your car heading to take care of him."

Michael had hated Brett from the start. The first time Trish brought him over, his face twisted in disgust. I elbowed him in the ribs and told him to act right or leave. He kept the peace for the rest of the night, but as soon as they walked out the door, he called him a wolf.

I had no clue what he meant, but every day

after that, he watched them like a hawk whenever we were all together.

He swore to me one day he would take off his sheep's wool and show his true self. I thought he was insane. Now I see he was the only one who saw the truth.

"I should have listened to you. I should have protected her. I should have protected you both." I let the tears drop down the sides of my face into my hair.

"I don't know how to not be mad that you left me, Michael. How am I supposed to live every single day knowing that you are never coming home?" The pain that comes with admitting that out loud drowns me. Ripping through my body so viciously. How do you accept you will never see someone again that was so deeply carved into your being? When the only reason you fought for your life was so they could have theirs. A life you struggle to believe they ever fought to live.

"You broke me. I fought for you every single day of my life and you didn't fight for me back."

Chapter Seven

Claire

It's been an entire week, and Trish still hasn't spoken to me. She is still sick, but refuses to let me take her to the doctor. I tried to ask about her back a couple days ago and she stormed away, locking herself in the room for the rest of the night.

"I'm sorry I'm so late today," I say, jumping into Layton's truck.

"It's okay. Gives me an excuse to not be working." He laughs. Not only has Trish not spoken to me, but it's also been a week since I heard from Tyler. Layton is great and I appreciate him softening the blow by making excuses that Tyler just has a lot going on. But I know he's avoiding me.

We are almost at the center when I realize I can't find my notebook. "Crap," I say, frantically

digging through my bag, hoping it appears.
"What's wrong?" he asks.

"I can't find my notebook. It's how I keep track of literally everything about work," I say, still desperately digging through my bag. Even though it's obviously not here, it's too late to go back. I can feel the truck making the turn into the parking lot.

"Today is group, right?" Layton asks, his voice sounding a bit off.

I sigh, giving up on my desperate search and looking over at him. His eyes locked ahead at the front of the building. I follow his gaze to the line that has formed in front of my door. At least twenty people are lined up waiting and the group doesn't even start for ten minutes.

"Oh, my gosh!" I say excitedly.

"Okay, I will run back and get your notebook. Do you know where you left it?" Layton asks. "Before you argue with me, you know I am going to win," he laughs.

"Fine, you are saving my ass. Thank you," I say, still staring at the line, a smile plastered on my face.

"Someone needs to do it," he says. "Now go get your ass up there and change some lives."

I smile at him, desperately wishing he was the one that made me feel something. He's gorgeous. Dark brown eyes, sharp jaw, muscular arms, but not a spark in sight. I jump from his truck, waving before walking up to the group.

"Good morning, Claire. I hope you don't mind. I brought some of my buddies along," Phillip greets, a smile tied into his words that didn't exist last week.

"I don't mind at all, Phillip; I'm actually so glad you did."

The group shuffles in, taking their seats, and I wait at the door, greeting the extra people that come through.

Layton's truck whips in and he jumps out, running me my notebook. A look marring his face that didn't exist ten minutes ago.

"Hey are you okay?" I ask, yelling across the lot.

"Yeah, I'm fine." He smiles. "Just work stuff. Don't you worry about me." He jumps back in the truck, waving before speeding out of the parking lot.

I walk over, taking my seat in the circle. Taking a second to look around at the faces. It's incredible to see so many new faces and I'm happy to see three from last week have returned, including Phillip.

"Hello, everyone, my name is Claire Andrews. As you may know, we have this group every Monday, and I have individual sessions available Tuesdays through Fridays. If anyone wants to stay after to set something up, feel free," I say. "Let's start by going around the circle. If you feel comfortable, please introduce yourself. Feel free to give as much or as little of your story as you'd like. If you do not want to share, no worries at all, you are more than welcome to just listen. When it gets to you, just say skip." My unofficial recruiter leads us off.

"Hello, my name is Philip Henderson. I was blessed enough to make it to the group last week. I have made a lot of mistakes in my life. Many, I didn't regret until recently. I was a firefighter in New York in 2001 when the towers fell. I lost a lot of brothers that day. I was twenty-five and full of a rage I had never felt before. My wife was pregnant with our daughter and begged me not to go, but she hadn't felt what it was like to help drag men I considered brothers through rubble, knowing they were already gone."

"That night I signed up for the United States Army. For the next nine weeks, I didn't see my wife because of training and then I deployed almost immediately when the war started." Phillip pauses, taking a deep breath before continuing.

"I kept telling myself that what I was doing was going to avenge my brothers' lives. I did not know the hell I was going to be thrown into. The towers falling were exactly what I lived, almost daily, for years. I missed my daughter's birth and pulled away from my wife almost completely. For eight years, I was in right up until the day I was caught in an IED explosion."

He pulls up his right pant leg, showing a metal rod. "I came home a different man. I ended up addicted to the painkillers and used alcohol to drown out the nightmares. My wife left me, and my daughter stopped calling me dad. I planned to let myself waste away. That's what I have done for the last fifteen years, anyway. A month ago, my phone rang, and it was my daughter. She said she just had her first child, and she wanted to know me, but on the condition that I got sober. We spent hours on the phone that night. After I hung up, I dumped every bottle of alcohol and pills in my house, and I have been sober ever since. The withdrawals were hell, but not like the hell of missing my daughter's childhood." He finishes brushing the tears from his cheeks.

"Phillip, I am so glad you are a part of this group. Getting sober is no simple task, and doing it alone is even harder. You should be so proud of yourself," I tell him.

We go around the circle. So many people, ages, and stories fill the room. Over the years, I've learned that addiction doesn't care who you are. Addiction feeds on the vulnerability of pain and it festers until it's so thick you feel you may never resurface. And some never do.

Chapter Eight

Tyler

I watch Earl gulp greedily at the lake. Today was brutal. Layton called out sick this morning, so double the work for me.

I pull my phone out of my pocket, a text from him lighting the screen from over an hour ago telling me he can't make it to pick up Claire today. It's already after three.

"Shit," I say, slamming my phone back in my pocket.

"Earl, let's go," I yell over to him. He stops his endless slurps and trots to my side. I waste no time flinging my leg over his back, and we take off back towards the truck.

The barn comes into view, and I ride up to one of the ranch hands.

"Can you get him unsaddled and put back in his stall for me?" I rush out, jumping from the horse's back, shoving his reins into the confused worker's hand.

"Boss, you good?" he shouts after me.

"Yeah, I'm fine. Thanks," I yell back, glancing down at my watch. She's already done.

The guilt is eating at me as I jump in my truck, shooting dirt behind me as I spin tires out of the driveway. I see her walking down the road and slow up alongside her. She looks up with a smile before dropping her brows into a scowl.

"I'm sorry. I thought you were Layton," she clips at me as she quickens her pace.

"Claire, wait. Please let me drive you," I shout out of the window, driving alongside of her.

"Actually, I think I am okay, but thank you for the offer," she says, increasing her speed.

I speed up to keep pace with her, throwing on my hazards.

"I am sorry, okay? I'm an idiot. I have no excuse for not coming to get you all week, I know, but I would really like to bring you home."

She stops, twisting to face me.

"Fine, drive me home since you obviously don't know how to take no for an answer," she says, throwing open my passenger door, jumping in, staring straight out the window.

"Claire—"

"No," she starts. "You know, I don't even know why I am so mad at you, but I am. I know I just met you. I know you've helped me over and over again, but you promised me. Not only that, but I told you no, and you still insisted on it. Then you let me down just like everyone else." She pauses. "Which, as I have said repeatedly, is stupid. I don't know you. You owe me nothing, but something about you felt different, and for the first time in my life, I thought about letting go. That's what I get for thinking you were Superman or Batman or who the heck ever." She laughs halfheartedly.

I clench my jaw. I know she is right. The drive is silent, just the sound of the gravel beneath the tires. I pull into her driveway and see her reaching for the handle. I gently grab her arm to explain myself.

"Claire, please. You're right, okay? I promised you and I let you down because I got freaked out. There aren't many people I will go out of my way for, especially not so damn fast." She turns and faces me. Her eyes lock on mine, sending my heart into a damn frenzy. I'm still touching her. "I have so much shit in my life. I honestly don't know if I have time for anything else."

Her face drops, and she rips her eyes away from mine.

"I understand," she whispers. "Hey, the good news is, how hard can it be to let go of something we never had, right?"

I move my hand from her arm up to her chin, gently forcing her to look at me again. I should leave it. She's right. We have nothing. We are two people that a few weeks ago didn't know each other's names. Yet the tension in the air between us feels like it could burn this whole damn town to the ground without a care.

Before I can think of an excuse, I press my lips into hers. She matches my every movement. I slide my tongue against the seam of her lips, and she lets me in. I savor the taste of her mint and honey.

Moving as close to her as I can so the center console is digging deep into my side. We both pause, foreheads pressed together with our steady breaths surrounding us.

"I'm still mad at you," she says, not bothering to pull away.

"That's fair. I am mad at me, too."

"Well, now it is going to be a lot harder to stomp out of this truck and never talk to you again. I think you just broke my brain," she says with a laugh.

"I don't deserve it, but do you think you could give me another chance? I promise I will pick you up. I won't be late. I won't ask Layton to do it for me. It will be me."

She leans back, seeming to think about it.

"Fine," she says, finally leaning away from me. "But if you lie to me again, that's it. I know you owe me nothing. If you aren't serious, tell me now. I won't expect another thing from you, but please don't promise me you will show up and just let me down again."

Part of me wants to run from her words. My mind screams that I am bound to mess everything up. I destroy everything I love. I ruin it. The logic says to let her out of the car. Let go of this ridiculous fantasy of happiness I am building in my mind. I accepted years ago I wasn't made for it.

Instead, I look her in those crystal blue eyes and promise I won't hurt her again. The lie effortlessly falling from my lips in a selfish hope it becomes the truth.

I don't even realize I am home until I turn into the driveway. I want nothing more than to collapse into bed, but I see Luke is up, sitting on the porch. The sun glittering off the cruel metal of the chair he's stuck in because of me. I bite back anger towards myself, knowing he deserves none of it, and climb from the truck.

"Hey," I say, walking up the steps. Dropping into the rocking chair next to him.

"The guys really pulled through," he says, staring at the now empty fields surrounding us.

"I know they did. I owe them all an apology and a bonus."

"Already added it to each of their checks for

this coming week."

"What about everyone else that came and helped?"

"They left with a case of fresh beef."

"About the other night," I say, eyes locked ahead. "I was an asshole. You are right, you may live here with me, but I can't remember the last time I actually had to help you do anything. I need to back off a bit."

"A bit?" he says sarcastically.

"Okay, a lot. I need to back off a lot," I say in defeat.

"I am glad you feel that way, because I actually have been waiting to talk to you." He pauses. I stay quiet, knowing what is about to come next won't be easy to hear.

"After our fight the other night, I started looking at houses. It ended up being a great idea because I found out the Bennets up the road are selling their house. Their oldest is also in a wheelchair, so the entire house has been modified to make it easier to live a normal life for someone like me," he says, and I can feel the excitement pouring out of him even though my heart is breaking. I know he is right. This could not be a better opportunity.

"Luke, that is amazing," I tell him honestly.

"That's not even the best part. When I put in my offer. They recognized my name and accepted immediately, saying they wanted to see it go to someone that could really benefit from everything in it. We go to closing next month."

I pause for a minute, realizing how quickly everything is about to change.

"I know this isn't easy on you, Tyler, but I hope you can understand and accept me leaving," he says, mistaking my silence for anger.

"I'm not upset. I'm going to miss having you around every day, but I am so proud of the man you are. You never needed me to take care of you. You are going to do amazing on your own. Just promise if you ever need something, you won't hesitate to ask."

"I won't. You will always be the first one I call," he replies, turning to head inside. "And, Tyler?"

"Yeah."

"I will always need you," he says before leaving me to stare in the distance.

Claire

"Have a great weekend," Phillip yells as he walks out the front door, the smile gracing his face growing more and more each time I see him.

He had been right about group. Each week, we have at least two new people. Phillip and some of the other members have been going around twice a week to nearby towns, seeing who they could help.

Once the room is empty, I shuffle through it, quickly gathering my things so I can meet Tyler. He has stuck to his word, picking me up and dropping me off every day for the last few weeks. Normally, still covered in dirt from the workday. Every day, he has a new picture of a baby cow for me to see.

As much as I wanted to hold a grudge for him abandoning me, it seems impossible. I know he is stretched thin with working on the ranch, but I am desperate for more of him than the quick conversations on the drive home and stolen kisses that drag on too long in my driveway every evening.

I know how insane this is. I barely know him. Before losing Michael, I would have never. I was always careful. There was no living, just surviving. Surviving just doesn't feel like it's enough anymore. I crave the butterflies, the excitement. I crave life.

The front door swings open. The youngest of the group, Mia, stops in front of me.

"Claire?" Her dark brown hair thrown up in a messy bun at the top of her head, with soft wisps framing her copper skin. Only seventeen, but I know the look of defeat carved deep into her green eyes because it's the exact look I saw in the mirror when I was her age.

"I'm so glad to see you could make it back out this week," I tell her. "Were you able to get the papers signed?"

"My parents still won't sign them," she bites out, shaking her head. "Only another week, and I won't need them, anyway. I'm not sure why I bothered the last couple of months."

"That's okay, the week will fly by. We've waited this long," I tell her reassuringly.

Mia has been the quietest in the group. Yet to share her story, she just sits in the back and seems to take it all in. She asked me day one about doing one-on-one sessions. I was excited, thinking it may be the only way for her to share, but week after week, her parents refuse to sign anything. The rules prevented me from doing more, and I didn't have any other choice but to follow them.

"Do you truly think people can overcome an addiction even if they seem too far gone?" she says thoughtfully.

"Over the years, I have had people stumble into meetings so high or drunk, they needed help to find a seat. I watched the same people collect their sobriety coins year after year. So yes, I believe there is a chance for anyone that wants to be helped," I tell her. "Is that what you think about yourself? That you're too far gone?"

"I like to believe I will never let myself get to that point," she says as my phone vibrates on the desk next to us. I quickly silence it, hoping she will continue, but I see her throw the walls back in place. "I better get going. I will see you next week."

I watch as she walks out the door before picking up the phone, Tyler's name lighting up the screen.

"Hey,"

"Did I interrupt?" he asks. "I just saw someone

run out, and I thought you'd be done, but now I feel like I ruined something."

I laugh. "Nope, we were just finishing up. She had to catch her ride, anyway." I pause, worry hitting me. "Is there a car here for her?" I ask.

Tyler gets quiet, then I hear his window lower and him yell out, asking if she has a ride. I can't hear her response.

"They must have left. She's talking about walking," he says.

I rush to the door without saying another word. "Mia, wait. We can drive you," I say, looking at Tyler with a question in my eyes.

He smiles at me. "Of course we can."

She pauses for a second before walking over to the truck.

"Mia, this is Tyler. Tyler, this is Mia."

"Hi," she says softly, refusing to look up. "Thanks for driving me. I promise I don't live very far. It's twenty-two East Way Road,"

"Thank you," I mouth to him. He just smiles back.

"So, how are all the baby cows making out?" I ask Tyler, hoping to break the awkward silence that has taken over the truck.

I see Mia instantly perk up in the mirror, her eyes shooting to the front.

"You have cows?" she asks.

"Yup, I own a ranch. We have a lot of different animals, but a lot of the cows are having babies this time of year."

"Wow, that's awesome," she says. "I used to want to be a veterinarian. I would love to work with farm animals one day."

"You could still become a vet," I encourage.

"I think that dream is gone," she says softly. "I had a scholarship lined up. I ended up losing it this year."

Her eyes drop to her hands that she's now twisting together in her lap.

"You never know," I tell her. "Maybe it won't be as easy to get now, but you don't seem like someone that gives up easily. I think you will find a way."

I see the small spark that lights behind her eyes. The tiny lift of her smile as she looks at me.

"Thank you, Claire," she says.

Tyler turns into her driveway. A beat-up trailer with trash littering the steps. The sound of raised voices carries from within as I look back at her. Mia seems unfazed as she grabs her bag from the floor and jumps from the truck.

"Are you going to be okay?" Tyler asks her. I can see the worry all over his face.

"I'm used to it," she says. "Thanks for the ride."

The door shuts, leaving us both in silence. I see Tyler fighting with himself as she pauses on the front step, taking a deep breath before going inside.

He backs the truck back into the street, anger marring his face.

"What do you have going on tonight?" he asks, finally breaking through the silence surrounding us.

"Nothing that I know of," I answer.

"Good," he says, turning the opposite way of my house. "I have something I want to show you."

It doesn't take long before we are pulling down a long dirt road lined with wire fencing.

"Welcome to the Magnolia Falls Ranch," he says, climbing from the truck.

I slide out, taking in the miles of open land surrounding me. Cows and horses running through their vastness. I didn't even realize Tyler has walked over to my side.

"It's breathtaking, isn't it? There are days I want nothing more than to just stand in the middle of it and never stop taking it all in."

"I have never seen anything like it," I answer, still in awe at the beauty surrounding me.

"I have something I want to show you," he says, grabbing my hand pulling me towards the large red barn alongside us. The smell of hay fills my senses. Once inside, he leads me forward to a closed stall.

"Look," he says, and I peek over the edge.

A tiny calf lays surrounded by piles of hay.

"Oh, my goodness!" I shout before realizing how loud I am.

"He was born yesterday morning. Unfortunately, his mama won't take to him." He wraps his arms around my shoulders, pulling me against his chest. "I have been trying to name him all day, but I just can't seem to think of anything. I was wondering if you would like to."

"Yes, I would love to." I try to think of something, but my mind goes blank. I want his name to be perfect.

"I think if you go in and pet him, it'll be easier to think of one." He smiles, opening the stall and walking me over to the calf's side. I gently lean down and pet his hair, earning me a soft grunt. "He is due for a bottle if you want to feed him. He is going to need lots of extra love without his mama."

"Absolutely, I would," I say.

"Well, if you are comfortable, you can keep saying hi, and I will make him up a bottle." I smile and nod as he heads out of the stall.

I gingerly kneel by my new friend.

"You good?" Tyler asks once I am settled.

"Better than good."

"I will be right over here. Making this up won't take long. If you need me, just yell."

"Hey, little buddy. My name is Claire. I promise I will take good care of you." He grunts at me, which I take as a thank you.

"Do you like the name Ohana?" I ask him. "There is a movie and they say Ohana means family, and family means nobody gets left behind. I think that is rather fitting for you."

I look up and see Tyler leaning over the stall door, smiling at me. "I see you picked a name," he says. "I think it's perfect."

He kneels beside me, placing the bottle in my hands and wrapping his hands around mine. That familiar spark shooting through me from his touch.

"Just hold the bottle like this." He leads my hands forwards and Ohana latches on. He lets my hands go, leaning back to watch. "See, you're a pro already."

"He has to be the cutest thing I've ever seen."

After Ohana slurps down the last of his bottle, he falls asleep. I tell him goodbye, and Tyler leads me back out of the barn. The endless fields that were just drenched in sunlight are now painted in a beautiful red and orange as the sun sinks in the sky.

"This is amazing, Tyler."

I watch in awe as the colors shift around us. The cows and horses grazing in the distant fields now silhouetted a fiery glow. The soft chirps of the birds around us shift to the sound of crickets and cicadas until the sun has disappeared, and we are blanketed in darkness.

"This is nothing," he says, wrapping me in his

arms, placing soft kisses on my temple. "There is so much more I want to show you."

I turn into his embrace, lifting on my toes to kiss him. My lips softly brush his until the softness isn't enough. The weeks of holding back seem to bubble over. Our touching becomes desperate as I lift, wrapping my legs around his waist. He pins me against the barn, the rough wood digging into my back and the undeniable feeling of him between my legs.

He trails his lips from my mouth down my neck and I cannot hold back the gasps that escape me as I grind against him. Desperate for the feeling clawing its way through me. He pulls back, locking eyes on me, searching for permission to go further. I nod, unsure of what I am agreeing to, and truthfully, not really finding it in me to care if this goes way too far. I am standing on the edge, ready to jump.

His fingers trail down my top, unbuttoning the buttons before freeing my breasts to the chill of the summer night. He follows the trail his fingers just took with his mouth, finally sucking me in. His fingers moving to the top of my leggings. He pauses again.

"I swear, Tyler, if you ask me if this is okay, I may cry. Please, go!" I cry out desperately between pants of breath. I am so close to falling.

His hand slips into my pants, moving my panties to the side before gently brushing over me. That's all it takes to push me over the edge. Fireworks burst behind my eyes. Tyler takes my mouth against his, swallowing my screams as he adds a finger deep inside of me, pulling every ounce of the orgasm from deep within me.

Tyler gently sets me on my feet, pinning me between him and the barn, his forehead against mine, our breath coming out in short pants.

"Holy shit," he says.

He grabs my face, pulling it up to look at him.

"That was the most amazing thing I have ever seen. I can't wait to have more of you," he whispers in my ear, placing a soft kiss on my lips.

I'm not sure how long we stay like that, making out under the stars surrounded by nothing but the sounds of crickets when his phone dings with a text.

He breaks away slowly, like he'd rather just ignore it, before slipping the phone from his pocket and reading the text. The glow from the screen showing his bruised lips and messy hair.

"Are you hungry?" he asks.

"Starved," I reply, struggling to pull myself away from the solid side of the barn.

"Great, my brother is making chili if you'd like to stay for dinner. I may be biased, but I swear he makes the best chili in the world," he says as we walk to his truck. He opens my door, helping me climb into my seat.

"I would love to."

I watch him walk around the front of the truck, wondering how the hell I am here. I have never felt this stable in my entire life. I say a silent prayer that I get to keep it.

Chapter Ten

Tyler

I pull up to the house, jumping out to help Claire from her side of the truck. I didn't tell Luke I was bringing anyone over. I honestly wasn't sure what my plan was, but when I walked back from making the bottle and saw her sitting on the ground talking to the calf like it was a tiny child, there was nothing I could do. I am in so deep with this girl already.

"Could I use the bathroom to freshen up?" Claire asks me as we walk through the front door.

"Third door on the left," I say, pointing down the hallway. "When you come out, just come back down the hall and I'll be right there through that opening," I tell her, pointing to the kitchen.

She smiles, giving me a quick squeeze before walking away.

Luke is in the kitchen cooking. He shoots me a grin when I walk in. "I hope you don't mind. I may have invited someone for dinner."

"Do tell me about this guest because I know that wasn't Layton, and he is the only person you have ever invited here before."

"Her name is Claire. She just moved here a couple of months ago from New York," I explain to him, hoping he can't read me as well as I know he can.

"So, what's the deal with her? You never bring anyone home and now you are not only bringing her here, but you came from the ranch," he asks, just as Claire walks in.

I shoot him a look, begging him to drop it.

"Claire, this is my brother Luke. Luke, this is Claire," I say, realizing I never mentioned the fact that he was in a wheelchair. It is so normal now I didn't even think.

"It is so great to meet you. Tyler has told me a lot about you over the last couple of weeks." She beams, not even taking a second to focus on anything but him. "Let me guess, he didn't tell you about me."

"He didn't, but you standing in our kitchen tells me plenty," Luke says, a huge grin covering his face. "It's nice to meet you. I hope you guys are hungry. I made a ton."

"I'm starving," Claire replies, fitting right in like she's meant to be here.

He dishes her a bowl and puts it in front of her on the counter.

She takes a huge bite.

"Luke, this is incredible."

"Thank you," he says. "It's my dad's famous recipe."

He dishes me out a bowl, and I smile. The nights Luke makes chili remind me of when everything was easier.

"Did you finish that test?" I ask.

"Yup, finished it this morning,"

"Luke is in college for his business degree," I tell Claire, unable to hide the pride I feel in that statement.

"Only a couple more months and I will be graduating. I did the accelerated courses, so I was able to get done quicker."

"I don't know how you do it. I struggled with keeping up with basic courses, accelerated would have killed me," she says.

"I'm pretty lucky. The work for the ranch is fairly simple, and Tyler helps a lot around the house. It gives me more time to focus on school," he tells her. "Really, Tyler has it way harder than me. I would hate working on the ranch every day. He is out there in all different weather all day long. Without him, dad's ranch would have crumbled."

"That's not true. You would have been just fine without me," I say. "Maybe even better off," I whisper under my breath.

The kitchen goes quiet. I get up from my chair and put my bowl in the sink.

"Why don't you guys go have a drink on the porch while I clean up," Luke says. "I got the dishes tonight."

"You cooked dinner," I argue.

"I can do them. You have company," Luke argues back.

"I don't mind helping with them." Claire adds in coming up behind me to put her plate in the sink. "I agree with Tyler. You cooked such a great dinner. Let us help clean it up."

"In that case, I do have a paper due this week I really should work on." He says.

"Go, we have this." She tells him reassuringly.

He locks eyes with me one more time, questions written in them.

"Luke, go do your paper." I tell him, leaving no room for argument.

"Fine, Claire, it was so nice to meet you." He says, leaving us in the kitchen with nothing but a thick tension surrounding us.

"It was great to meet you, too." She yells after him while grabbing the wash rag and soap to start scrubbing the dishes.

"You okay?" she asks as she hands me the dish to dry. I don't answer.

"Your brother seems really nice," Claire says handing me another dish.

"He is."

"It is amazing that he could complete a four-year degree in two while doing physical therapy. Seriously. I can't imagine it was easy to get that focus back after an accident that severe." I feel the memories clawing to get free, but I push them down. Luke told Claire he was in an accident, but nothing more about what really happened that day or how I was the reason behind it.

"Hey, seriously, are you okay?" I look down and see Claire grasping my hand I have tightly clenched on the counter.

"Yeah, I'm fine." I fake a laugh. "I just remembered I have to be at the ranch early tomorrow to patch a couple fences."

She looks at me like she is trying to read the truth in my words. I wrap her in a hug. "I promise I'm okay," I lie thankfully, she drops it leaning into me.

"Well, in that case, I guess it's time for me to get back home. I have to feed Charlie. He is just starting to sneak from under the couch and steal food from the bowl when I am away." She smiles and I can't help but smile back. "I am also happy to report I think his hair may be coming back. I can't be sure, but it looks promising."

She dries her hands and continues to fill me in on Charlie and we walk to my truck. I let her. Using every word to convince myself I am not wrong by not being honest with her tonight. I know when she finds out the truth, this will be done. How can it not? Guys like me don't deserve happiness.

Chapter Eleven

Claire

The ride home was quiet. Tyler seemed to answer everything with a simple yes or no. I know there is more going on than he's willing to share, but I understand that more than most. As much as I want to pry for more, I know it's better to let him tell me when he's ready.

I jump out of the truck. He follows behind me, walking up the front steps before unlocking it. I pause, turning to him. He locks me in a stare, walking me back to the door. He leans in, taking my mouth into his. It feels like an hour passes before he finally breaks the kiss, leaning his head against mine.

"I hate that you can't stay," I tell him.

"I hate that I can't stay too. This should be the last few days of craziness on the ranch for a bit then I can take you out on a real date."

I smile at him, and he kisses me softly one more time before stepping away. The cool late summer air hitting the places he just warmed.

"Claire?" he asks.

"Hmm?" I reply softly.

"Do you think we are friends yet?"

I laugh, leaving his question hanging in the air as I walk through the door.

The house is quiet and dark. Trish isn't home, not that she wouldn't just avoid me, anyway. I watch the closed door across the hall. The room I have so easily avoided for weeks somehow draws me towards it.

I stop, my hand on the handle, debating on turning around, but I push through swinging open the door. The moon shining through the blinds casts just enough light to see, so I don't bother with the light. I walk over, grabbing a box from the top of the pile, before carrying it to the living room plopping it on the glass coffee table.

The box somehow seems less menacing than it did a few weeks ago. I pull apart the top, looking inside at the stack of items. A pile of papers, a blue toy car, and a random stack of photos. I grab them out, my hands trembling.

Michael stares back at me. He is about ten. His face completely covered in chocolate ice cream as Trish looks at him smiling. I remember every second of that day. I had just gotten my license, and we decided to take Michael for ice cream. He swore he was big enough to finish the monster sundae. After a valiant effort, most of the sundae was no more than a puddle of melted mess. It was one of the few times life felt carefree.

I reach up, swiping away a tear that escaped my eye when light shines through the house capturing my attention from a car that pulled into the driveway. I figure they must be turning around since they disappear a few seconds later, but then the front door opens quietly and Trish walks in.

She sees me on the couch and pauses, taking in the open box in front of me.

"I knew you could do it," she says softly.

"You were right. I think I just needed some more time. I was so afraid seeing his stuff would make it harder to heal," I say, placing the photo back inside of the box. "I think I actually need this, though."

A soft smile flashes across her face. I am waiting for her to walk right by. My heart braces to accept the pain of being shut out once again. Instead, she rushes over to me, dropping on the couch and throwing her arms around me. I wrap her tightly in my arms, instantly bursting with tears.

"The car is done. Layton finished it a little while ago, but it's still at the ranch," she says softly. "He fixed it for just the cost of parts."

I sit up.

"I thought the car was dead. I didn't even know Layton was fixing it for us." She hesitates, looking around the room.

"Yeah, well, that day he came to get your notebook. He said he would drive over to the shop and take a look. She's as good as new now."

"I pull my phone out. How much was it? I will send over the money now," I tell her.

"Claire, please don't. I have been such a bad friend. The least I could do is pay for the car. You didn't second guess bringing me here with you, and I just shut you out the first chance I got. I am so freaking sorry," she says between sobs. "I just. There are some things you don't know, and I don't know if I am ready to talk about them, but please know I am okay. I am safe now."

I realize she is talking about her ex, and my blood boils at the thought of him.

"You don't have to talk. I am here for you, no matter what. Please know that," I say to her, tears spilling from my eyes.

"I have been such an awful friend." She cries.

"You have not. I didn't even realize how badly you had been hurt. I feel so bad that I missed all the signs."

"It's not your fault. It didn't start getting bad until after your brother started struggling again. You were doing everything you could to save him, which is exactly where you needed to be."

Charlie picks this moment to come out from under the couch, jumping on top of us and purring.

Trish and I look at each other in shock, afraid to talk and scare him away. She reaches out first, gently petting his half patchy back. We hold our breaths, waiting to see his reaction. He responds by purring louder and leaning into her.

"Maybe you're not so bad, Charlie," she says softly, pulling him to her chest.

The sound of my phone ringing pulls me from my sleep. I am still on the couch, Trish's head laying against my chest, Charlie tucked safely on her lap still wrapped tight in her arms.

I gently pull myself out from under them, somehow managing not to wake them up and grab my phone from the coffee table, Tyler's name lighting up the screen.

"Hey," I answer.

"I got done earlier than I thought today, and I was wondering if you were busy?" he asks.

"I have nothing going on today," I reply, walking into the kitchen to start a pot of coffee.

"Awesome. I was hoping you may want to come over to the ranch for the day?" he asks. "I could pick you up in an hour?"

"An hour is perfect," I reply.

"Great, I have something planned that I think you are going to love. I will be there soon."

I hurry into my room, getting a quick shower and tossing on some jeans and a t-shirt, hoping that the plan entails the ranch. Then head back into the kitchen to get myself a cup of coffee.

"Good morning," Trish yawns from the couch.

"Hey, would you like some coffee? I was just pouring a cup?"

"Yes, please."

I pour her a mug, adding cream and sugar before handing it to her. "Claire I—" she's cut off by the sound of a knock on the door.

"You, okay?" I ask her.

"Yeah, I was just going to say thank you for everything. I am really glad I have you in my life." Another knock. "You should probably get that. It's probably that cowboy." She winks.

I swat at her and walk over, opening the door.

"You're early," I say, but I am greeted by Mia. Tears streaking down her cheeks.

"I am so sorry. I didn't know where else to go. I asked Mrs. Shirley at the bakery if she knew where you lived. She knows everything about everyone, ya know, and she told me, so I ran all the way here," she cries as she throws her arms around my waist.

I look back at Trish. She looks unsure if she

should stay or go. I motion I am okay, and she gives me a soft smile, whispering to call her if I need her.

"Mia, what happened?"

"This morning they got mad and threw all my stuff in the front yard. I didn't know where else to go."

I wrap her in my arms, unsure of what to say.

We are still standing in the open door when Tyler pulls in. He wastes no time jumping from the truck running to our side.

"What happened?" he asks.

"They kicked me out," Mia cries.

He returns my gaze with the same expression. A silent question of *what the hell are we going to do?*

"Should I invite her with us for the day?" he mouths over her head.

"It's okay with me if it is with you," I mouth back.

"Hey," he says, putting a soft hand on Mia's shoulder. "How would you feel about coming to the ranch with Claire and I today? I could really use the extra hand."

Mia pulls back, wiping her tears on the back of her arm.

"Are you sure? I don't want to butt in on your guys' day?" she asks softly.

"Yes, I am sure. What would be better than getting to show you all the animals on the ranch? That is one of your dreams, right?" Tyler asks.

"Claire?" She turns to me with a question.

"Absolutely. I would love you to come," I say to her reassuringly. "Plus, there's someone there I think you're going to want to meet."

I walk her to Tyler's truck, still wrapped in my arm, helping her into the back.

"Would you mind if we stopped really quickly at my house so I can grab a bag?" she asks.

"No problem, it's on the way," Tyler says, pulling out of the driveway.

We pull up to her house, the front yard scattered with Mia's belongings. She jumps out quickly, grabbing a book-bag discarded in the mess, shoving things inside of it when the front door of the rundown trailer swings open.

A woman steps out, her hair slicked with grease and pick marks covering most of her olive skin.

"I told you to leave," the woman shouts. Tyler and I both jump from the truck, putting ourselves between Mia and who I am assuming is her mother.

"Oh, you brought friends, I see. Is this the woman who made you think you were better than us, Mia?" the woman mocks, looking me up and down in disgust. "Good, you want her? Keep her," she shouts, slamming the door.

Mia quickly stuffs the bag; Tyler and I help as much as we can before throwing random stuff in the bed of Tyler's truck. Her mom walks back through the door, staring at us.

"Just leave the rest. I got what I needed," she says, tears streaking her face as she takes in the rest of her stuff discarded like trash in the yard.

Tyler shoots me a look somewhere between 'heartbroken' and 'I may lose it on her mom'. I feel the same way. I want nothing more than to tell Mia's mother what a huge mistake she is making, but I know it won't help. I help lift Mia to her feet, grabbing the book-bag from her hand and tossing it in the truck before helping Mia back into her seat, then getting into my own.

I look back at Mia's mother. "You know my entire family is dead." I hear Tyler suck in a breath. "Everyone I have ever loved is gone. I would kill to have my mom and brother back, and here you are with a beautiful, smart daughter that loves you. Yet you are tossing her out of your life without a second thought."

With that, I climb in the truck as Tyler jogs around the front, staring at me before staring at the engine and driving off. I stare out the window, fighting the tears. Angry tears that a mother could be so cruel.

"Claire," Mia says quietly as we pull into the ranch.

"Yes?"

"I am sorry about your family," she says.

"It's okay," I reply. "I miss them every day, but I know I need to live for them." Tyler looks over at me, a sympathetic smile on his face.

"Mia," I say, jumping from the truck. "Welcome to Magnolia Falls ranch." She jumps out behind me, looking around.

"This is the most beautiful thing I have ever seen," she gushes.

"This isn't even the best part," Tyler says as he walks up to us. "Follow me."

Tyler leads Mia into the barn to meet Ohana. I follow behind, watching the two of them baby talk to the tiny cow. Once he has her set up with a bottle, he walks over to me.

He leans into my side. "So, you have a plan?"

"Not even close to one," I reply as we stare at the girl in front of us.

"I have to go back and get the rest of her stuff. I can't just leave it sitting out there," he says to me.

"I hated leaving all of that behind. She was so heartbroken," I say to him. "Are you sure you will be okay going back there?"

"Yeah, I am going to get a couple of guys on the farm to come with me. We can leave it in my one barn until she has a permanent place to go."

"I feel like I should let her live with me, but I'll be violating so many rules in doing that," I tell him. "I can't just let her go out on the street, though. I really care about her, Tyler."

"I know. I care about her, too."

"I'm going to call my boss. See what she thinks I should do," I say.

He smiles at me. Wrapping his arm around my waist.

"I'll be back soon. Head inside, Luke made lunch," he says before kissing me goodbye.

"So, is Tyler your boyfriend?" Mia asks, breaking me from the fog of watching him walk away.

"I am not sure what he is to me," I answer honestly.

Part of me craves something serious. I am constantly reminded of that with every wedding announcement on social media from someone I went to school with. On the other hand, I am loving the simplicity of not having a label on whatever this is. That way, if it blows up in my face, maybe it will be easier.

"Claire, can I tell you something, and you promise not to be mad at me?" I look over at her standing next to me. She is locked in on the door and my heart drops.

"You can tell me anything, Mia," I tell her sincerely.

"I am not addicted to anything. I have never even touched anything like that in my life," she says, looking up at me, her eyes full of unshed tears.

I let her words sink in.

"I lied because I thought if I came, I could understand my parents. Maybe help them," she whispers.

I open the stall door between us, going over to wrap my arms around her.

"Oh, Mia, I am so sorry you couldn't help your parents. I know how hard it is trying to save someone you love from addiction. Sadly, you can't help someone that doesn't want to be helped," I tell her, tears filling my eyes. "You don't know how happy I am that you are not really struggling, though."

"I know that. I didn't want to believe it, though," she says. "All of that just to learn they have been planning to kick me out the day I turned eighteen for years," she says, collapsing against my chest.

I freeze, realizing today is her birthday. She's eighteen. My mind races with if this could mean she can stay with me.

"Mia," I say, wrapping her tightly in my arms. "I'm so sorry I didn't even realize. Happy birthday. I know this is probably not the birthday you planned, but I promise we will figure something out. I refuse to let you go without a place to stay."

She pauses, smiling down at Ohana in her lap. "I actually think it's better."

I pull her back in against me. Her head dropping on my shoulder. For the first time since I met her, she looks unguarded. I silently promise myself I will somehow give her the future she deserves to have. A promise I may not be able to keep, but I will fight like hell to make it true.

Chapter Twelve

Tyler

I stare out the window, watching Layton packing the last few things in Mia's yard. Thankfully, no one was here when we arrived. I'd much rather still be out there with him loading up this truck than listening to the ring through the phone against my ear.

"Tyler?" My mom's voice comes over the line in a whisper.

I sit in silence, unsure what to say or why I even made this call. I've put my mom through hell and the first time I call her in years is to ask her for a favor. It leaves a bitter taste in my mouth, but I know my mom will know what to do for Mia.

"Hey, mom," I reply, finally swallowing my pride.

She audibly sucks in a breath. The weight of how I've treated her smacking me in the gut, full force.

"Oh, Tyler, I never thought I would hear your voice again. You haven't returned my calls in so long," she chokes out.

"I know, mom," I tell her sincerely. "I'm sorry. I just—"

"I know what you think, Tyler, but you are not protecting me by cutting me from your life. You are killing me," she cries.

Again, I say nothing. My throat is too thick to speak. The last thing I want to do is hurt her, but I'll be damned if I can figure out how to stop.

"Tyler, what's wrong? Do you need help?" she asks.

"I'm so sorry. I don't know who else to call. I know it's messed up to call you after all of this time for a favor, but you are the best woman I know, and I need a safe place for someone," I say, keeping my emotions in check.

"You can always call me. I'm your mother. There is nothing I wouldn't do for you."

"Her name is Mia. She is seventeen and her family just kicked her out. She's a nice girl, just a bit off track. I just don't want her out on the street. It would destroy Claire if something happened to her," I explain.

"Well, you know I have the extra space. Bring her over. She is welcome as long as she needs a place to stay," she tells me. "And Tyler please, I am begging you not to cut me out anymore. What happened is done. That day was the worst day of my life and not because your brother lost his ability to walk, but because I feel like my other child died that day. The worst part is I mourn him daily, and he's still very much alive. I need that son back, Tyler. I need you."

"I know, mom," I tell her. "I love you. I will be there soon."

I hang up, chucking my phone to the ground before taking my frustration out on the steering wheel. I don't know how long I sit there, but next I know, Layton is leaning across the center console, bear hugging me to stop.

"What the hell, man? What happened?" he says between breaths.

"Oh, it's all great. She's going to take Mia because she's a saint, and I'm still here, breaking her damn heart like the massive piece of shit I am," I say, slamming my hand through my hair. "I don't know how to get this right."

"Dude, your mom loves you and has never blamed you. You need to stop avoiding her at some point. I think this is good for you."

I know he's right, but I still sulk in silence all the way home.

When I walk into the house, Claire and Mia are in the kitchen with Luke. Instantly, I feel lighter when I see Claire laughing at something Luke said. He looks up, realizing I am there.

"Hey, look who finally decided to show up," Luke says, smiling.

"Luke has been telling us all about his new house," Claire says.

"I just have to make sure I still come to feed him once or twice a week. I am worried he may forget he needs food and wither away without me." He laughs until he locks eyes on me, and his laugh is replaced with a worried look. "You want some food?"

"Thanks, man, but I'm really not hungry," I tell him, earning me an even bigger look of concern. "Claire, can I talk to you really fast?"

She shoots up quickly from her seat and follows me into the side room.

"What happened?" she whispers.

"Nothing. No one was there. We got everything. I wanted to talk to you about where Mia is going to go."

She deflates in front of me.

"I called my boss. She said I'd definitely be blurring the lines with work, and she doesn't advise it, if it can be avoided," she tells me. "I don't know what else to do though."

"Do you think her parents will report her as a runaway?" I ask, not wanting to put my mom in any harm.

"Today's her birthday," she says, deflating. "I seriously hate them so much that they would kick her out on her birthday."

"I think I have a solution. I called my mom. She said she is welcome to stay with her as long as she needs to," I say, causing her to let out a squeak, wrapping her arms around me.

"Are you serious? Tyler, that would be amazing. Thank you so much!" She pauses, looking at me. "What's wrong?"

"Nothing, I am just tired from the day. You're right, it is great news. My mom's an amazing woman, and I know she will watch out for her. We should probably go see if it's okay with Mia before it gets too late, so we can get her over there if she wants to go."

Claire runs into the kitchen, and I follow behind, trying my best to hide the anxiety clawing through me.

"Mia, it's up to you, but Tyler and Luke's mom said it would be okay if you stayed with her for a while," she says.

I feel Luke's eyes dart towards me, and I shoot him a look. We stay locked in a silent battle until Mia throws her arms around me, breaking my focus.

Chapter Thirteen

Claire

Mia has Tyler wrapped in a hug. I know she's crying. Tyler freezes, looking at me like he's unsure of what to do before he wraps his arms around her, too.

I look over at Luke, who is still silently sitting beside me, staring at Tyler, a look I can only describe as shock written on his face.

"Is everything okay?" I whisper. I feel Tyler's stare locked on us and can hear Mia still talking to him about his mom's house. His answers have changed from detailed explanations to only clipped 'yes' or 'no' responses.

"Everything's great," Luke says, finally looking at me. "So, Tyler, when are you heading to moms?"

Tyler rubs his hand across his jaw. I can feel the tension in the room.

"What's wrong?" I ask softly. I look over at Mia, who just shrugs her shoulders back at me.

"Everything is fine," Tyler huffs. "Let's head over before it gets too late."

With that, he grabs his keys from the counter and walks out to the truck; the door shutting loudly behind him. Not even waiting to see if we have followed behind.

"Maybe this isn't a great idea," Mia says meekly, looking at the floor as she kicks at nothing.

"No, this is a great idea, I promise. My mom is going to be over the moon to have someone at the house with her. She gets lonely, and you guys are going to get along great." Luke smiles reassuringly.

We walk out to Tyler's truck. Mia jumps in the back, and I climb into the passenger side. Tyler says nothing as he shifts into drive and pulls down the dirt driveway toward the main road. I reach across, putting my hand on his leg. He looks up at me once we stop at a red light. The war behind his eyes almost makes me want to look away, but I stay locked on him.

"I'm sorry," he whispers.

"You don't have to tell me, but thank you for doing this for her," I whisper back.

He shoots me a smile. His eyes locked on the rear-view.

"Mia, I promise my mom is the most amazing woman you will ever meet. She is going to love you. She has a dog. He is a Newfoundland named Goose. He's a giant but super sweet." I watch her instantly light back up.

"Oh my gosh, are those the ones that look like bears?" she asks excitedly.

"Yup," he says, turning on his blinker, "and you are not far from either Claire or my house. If you ever need anything or want to come to the ranch, give Claire a call and we can come and pick you up." He turns onto a road lined with trees. "You see that mailbox that looks like a little yellow house?"

She nods her head yes.

"That is where you are going to be staying." He smiles as we pull into the driveway of a beautiful two-story light-yellow house.

The front door flies open before he has even shifted it into park. A giant black bear runs through the front door, followed by a woman with flowing dark brown hair.

"Oh, my goodness!" Mia cries before jumping from the truck, wrapping Goose in a giant hug. Tyler's mother laughs, joy lighting her face. She walks from the porch down to Mia, who is now standing in the middle of the yard. Tyler has yet to move. I turn back to face him, softly grabbing his face, sure the tint on his windows is enough to hide us. He continues to stare past me.

"Tell me what to do, Tyler," I whisper to him, causing him to lock eyes with me.

"I haven't seen my mom in over a decade," he says, pain lacing his words.

Shock hits me at how huge this moment is, and questions race through my mind.

He leans in to kiss me. "Let's do this," he says, leaning back, taking one more deep breath, then jumping from the truck.

I follow behind him, watching his mom turn to the sound of our doors closing. Her eyes lock on him across the yard. I see her break before my eyes, but she pulls herself back together before slowly taking a step towards him. Seeming afraid if she moves too quickly, he may jump back in the truck and speed off for another decade.

"Hey, mom," he says as the gap between them closes. She takes that as her invitation and runs crashing into him. She is so much smaller than him, maybe five-foot-three and can't weigh more than a hundred and twenty pounds. She all but disappears when he wraps his arms around her.

"Oh baby, you do not know how happy I am to see you," she chokes out. They stay wrapped in a hug for a minute before she gently pulls away, locking eyes on me. Her eyes are the same shade of green as Tyler's, but everything else about her screams Luke.

"Mom, this is Claire. My—" He awkwardly pauses, glancing at me like he didn't think this far ahead. "Friend?" he finishes as a question.

His mom lets out a laugh.

"Well, it's great to meet you, Claire. Tyler's friend." She winks at the last part.

"You know your dad was also my," she throws her fingers up in air quotes, "'Friend' for a while. You can call me Pam, honey."

I laugh. I should probably feel awkward, but watching Tyler pick up so easily with his mom after all this time makes it hard. I thought there would be tension and awkwardness, but it seems as if they have never missed a second.

We all look across the yard to where Mia plays with Goose. His gigantic body running after a yellow tennis ball she just tossed across the yard. She has a smile stretched across her face, bigger than I have ever seen.

"How can a parent willingly give that up?" Pam says sadly. I feel Tyler inch closer to me.

"It seems her parents are really struggling with addiction. Mia joined my group and pretended she was the one struggling to figure out how to save them," I say, matching her tone.

Tyler turns sharply to face me. "What?"

"Yup, she said she's never actually done anything," I tell him and watch as he noticeably relaxes. "She just wanted to save her parents. When she tried to show them what she learned in the group sessions, they got angry and kicked her out."

I see the rage in his eyes.

"Good, she deserves better than them," he says angrily. "I'm going to go talk to her."

I look over at his mom as she stares at him, walking away.

"He has changed so much since I saw him last. He was so angry for all the wrong reasons and lost all his passion for life. I can't tell you how amazing it is to see him care about something," she says, her words filled with a pain that matches her eyes.

I shoot her a sad smile, realizing I know almost nothing about Tyler's past at all. It seems anytime we head to that territory, he shuts the conversation down immediately. My mind drifts to the accident that Luke was in, realizing he didn't even give me any details beyond the fact that he was in a car accident when he was thirteen. After that, he went right into talking about college.

"Hey." Tyler's voice breaks through my thoughts. "I'm going to start bringing in stuff before it gets too dark. I sent Mia in with my mom." I look beside me and realize not only is Tyler's mom gone, but the sky is shifting to orange.

"I'll help," I say, walking towards the truck. We carry in arms full of stuff over the next hour racing the sun on the horizon, but still have to grab the last of it with a flashlight in the pitch black. His mom and Mia ask multiple times if they can help, but Tyler immediately dismisses them. He argues I should stay in too, but I ignore him.

I drop the last bag onto the bed and see another get tossed alongside it. Mia and his mom's laughter trails up the steps from the living room where they are still both sitting, having the time of their lives.

Warmth fills the space behind me, and I turn into Tyler, who has caged me in against the bed. The green in his eyes is only a thin line around his pupils. I feel the heat course through me before he has even touched me. I swear, when his fingers finally trace down my arm, I almost combust.

"I don't know how much longer I can be in this house today," he tells me honestly, leaning his forehead against mine.

"I guess we should get you back home, then," I say. He leans in, taking my lips against his. It's not a rushed kiss, more of one he is hoping takes away the pain.

Our goodbyes are kind of rushed, but his mom doesn't seem to mind. She smiles wide, wrapping him in her arms too tightly. I fear she may break him, which causes me to chuckle since she is so tiny. He promises her she will see him at Luke's housewarming in a couple of weeks and she cries as we leave.

The first few minutes of the ride are silent; my brain is anything but.

"I have made some choices in my life that I am far from proud of, Claire. I won't lie and let you think I am a saint, because that is so far from the truth," he says, pain wrapped in his words. "As much as I would love to tell you all of it, I just don't have it in me right now."

"You don't have to tell me," I say softly, even though I want him to. I want him to give me all of his pain so I can try my damnedest to fix it. His pain fills the car so thick I can feel it in my soul. I realize unless he wants me to be a part of that pain, there isn't a damn thing I can do to lessen it.

He pulls the truck down his driveway, shifting into park.

"It's getting really hard to keep my hands off of you, Claire," he says huskily, leaning in against my ear. "I want to rip those tight-ass pants off and taste every inch of you right now and it's killing me that I can't."

I moan embarrassingly loud at the thought, and he doesn't waste a second leaning forward, taking my lips against his.

He breaks the kiss, leaning his head against mine. "Can you please stay with me tonight?" he asks, his voice verging on desperate. I realize even though seeing his mom went well today, it has taken a ton out of him.

"I would love that," I tell him sincerely, because I want nothing more than to spend tonight with him, and so many more after that. I feel like I am already losing a battle I know I can't win. Tyler has promised me nothing. No future, no look into his past. If anything, he has kept every part of him under lock and key, but has still somehow sunk deep into my bones. My mind whispers, *I am falling in love with this man*, but I quickly shut down the thought.

He hops from the driver's seat, shutting the door. Nervous energy courses through me as I watch him walk around the front of the truck towards my side.

My door is ripped open, and his hands are on me in an instant. Sliding through my hair, tilting my head at the perfect angle to allow him to devour me. His tongue battles with mine as he tugs me to my feet outside. Somehow shutting the door behind me, my back colliding with the cool metal frame, and he leans into me. His hands reach under my thighs, giving me the invitation to jump up and wrap them around his hips.

He leans forward again, my body pinned between the hard metal behind me and his hard body, and he grinds against where I desperately want more of him. The hardness of the truck on my back is replaced with the cool summer night air as he carries me towards the house. Never missing a beat as his tongue still battles against mine.

The sound of the door closing breaks through the thick fog that's wrapped through my body and I tug at his shirt to rip it over his head as he does the same with mine. His hands instantly come up to cup my breast as he leans me against the wall. I use the moment to begin working on the button of his jeans, desperate to feel more of him. My hands skim up his stomach once I have them undone to a patch of rough skin which causes him to suck in a breath.

I try to pull back to look at him, but he leans back in, capturing my mouth against his again. I quickly store the questions in the back of my mind for later and lose myself in him as he carries me to his room and drops me on his bed.

The room is blanketed in darkness with only the moonlight to silhouette our bodies as it peeks through the curtains. He pulls my jeans down my legs, climbing back up my body, peppering kisses up my thighs until he reaches my center, kissing through the thin black lace that covers me.

I moan as I rake my hands into his hair, desperately pulling him closer.

He wastes no time ripping my panties down my legs and tossing them across the room without looking as his mouth descends on me. His tongue does something against my clit that is making lights shoot behind my eyes. I pull his hair to get him even closer while my legs fight to push him away.

It's so good. It's too much. It's everything and unlike anything I have ever felt before.

Every inch of me is on edge—like a live wire, seconds from burning down the entire city. Then he pushes a finger in me, curling it to just the right spot and his mouth latches back over my clit, sucking.

I am gone. I know I am moaning like a feral animal, but I can't hear it. I am shooting through the sky surrounded by fireworks, then floating back to the bed where Tyler stands, ripping off his pants while he bites the corner of a condom wrapper.

I take a minute to appreciate every inch of him. His toned arms and shoulders down his stomach, which is all six-pack muscle and that V everyone talks about. A deep raised scar across it all, but I don't stop. I follow down the V right to him, sliding the condom over the biggest penis I have ever seen in real life. A sound of shock must escape me because he chuckles.

"You okay?" he asks, climbing on the bed over top of me.

"Yup, completely fine," I say. "One thing, though, that thing may not work." He pauses and stares at me.

"It may not work?" he asks, confused.

"Yeah, it's not going to fit," I tell him seriously. He looks shocked at my response, and I realize the men I have been with in the past have been less than endowed. I still feel like he is more blessed than most.

"Okay," he whispers. "How about this? I go really slow, and if at any point it's too much, I'll stop."

"Okay," I tell him, and he crashes his lips against mine. I get lost in his kiss and he slowly begins to push inside of me. I gasp and he stops, but I dig my nails into his ass, pushing him to keep going.

Finally, he fills me completely. Pausing to break the kiss and capture my eyes again.

"You alright?" he says, his voice strained.

"Please," I cry out, "Please move or I might die."

"Oh, thank God," he says as he pulls his hips back and pushes back into me over and over again.

I can't even think straight. It has never felt like this. Hell, I would have been fine never having sex again before this, but I know this will ruin me. His mouth goes to my neck, gently sucking his way down to my breast, where he pulls my nipple deep into his mouth, causing electricity to shoot through me once again.

He doesn't stop, though. He brings his hand to my clit, making soft circles as he continues to suck and thrust into me. It's all too much. My mind goes blank. I am nothing but a moaning pile of ecstasy, and his thrusts become faster and less rhythmic. I hear his moan before he stills inside of me.

He slowly pulls out, leaning over to kiss me one more time before he gets up to throw away the condom. I lay unable to move. My body hums, or maybe it's buzzing like I'm high. It's like nothing I ever felt, and I want more of it.

Do not get attached, Claire; he hasn't promised you anything. I scold myself as he walks back into the room, holding a washcloth in his hand.

I shoot him a confused look, but he gently goes to open my legs and wipe me off. There is nothing my mind can do now. My heart is in deep, and I am afraid of how badly this is going to hurt when I surface.

I must have fallen asleep because the next thing I know, the smell of bacon overcomes my senses. I slowly open my eyes to reveal the sun streaming through the blinds, landing on the empty spot beside me. Slowly sitting up, I take in Tyler's room. A few trophies sit on his shelf next to a couple of pictures of him and Luke.

Standing up with his sheet tightly wrapped around my chest, I walk over, running my finger along the picture of Luke in a graduation cap and gown. Tyler has his hand on his shoulder, grinning down at his brother, his face full of pride.

"He graduated top of his class." Tyler's words jolt me out of my trance, and I turn to see him leaning against the door frame, smiling at me, dressed in a tight, white t-shirt and dark blue jeans with his hair still damp from a shower.

"You both look so happy," I say, turning back to take in the photo one more time before making my way towards him, letting him wrap me in his arms.

"It has been a crazy couple of years for us, but that doesn't take away the fact that we love spending time together." His fingers run down my hair, tracing under my chin, and he tilts my face up towards him. "I have a hot bubble bath ready for you. Your clothes are washed and on the counter. There's a spare toothbrush and toothpaste right beside that. When you're done, a nice hot breakfast will be on the table," he whispers before leaning in and capturing my lips with his.

"Where did you come from, Tyler Henry?" I say as I rest my forehead against his.

He leans in and kisses my nose. "I could say the same thing to you. Before you not-so-gracefully stumbled your way into this town, I didn't even know girls like you existed." With that, he bends down, giving me another short peck before turning to walk away. "Go get in the tub. I'm going to finish breakfast." He shoots me a quick smile before leaving the room.

Chapter Fourteen

Tyler

How hard can it be to make an omelet?

I think as I look at the five different recipe books spread out on the counter in front of me that mom sent over with Luke. Claiming if I order out every time he didn't cook, I was going to weigh 600 pounds.

Mushrooms? No, they are too risky, maybe tomatoes?

I grab a plump, bright red tomato and set it on the counter next to the eggs and cheese. I check on the bacon in the frying pan and turn on a pot of coffee.

I've got this.

"Something smells yummy." The sweet words fill my ears and I turn to see Claire walking into the kitchen. Her hair, still wet from the bath, hangs down past her shoulders. She has on her now clean clothes from yesterday and she looks incredible.

Are you just going to stare, or are you going to feed me some of this delicious food you've cooked?" she laughs, her lips curling into a smile.

I turn to make her a plate. "It's kind of hard not to stare. You look absolutely beautiful this morning." With that, I put a plate in front of her and watch her lean in and take a bite. A soft moan fills the room. "Darling, you are going to have to not do that again, or I may be tempted to take you right back to bed and completely forget all the plans I've made for us today."

She blushes, "Well, I can't say I would be completely upset with that, though I am intrigued by these plans." She leans in and takes another bite. "I thought you said you couldn't cook? This is incredible."

"You can thank *Amazing Meals in Minutes* for that," I say, pointing towards the book that made this all happen. "Though it should say 'in an hour' because there is no way someone can do all this in minutes." I walk over, putting the books away and finish washing the last dish of the dozens I soiled.

Taking her last bite, she stands up and walks over to me, wrapping her arms around my waist. "Well, I think you did a great job. Thank you so much for everything this morning. You really are amazing." She leans up and places a kiss on my cheek.

"It isn't over yet. Come on, I have something I want to show you before Mia gets here," I tell her.

"Mia is coming!" she says excitedly, jumping up to throw on her sneakers.

"Yup, I have a couple of the guys that are going to teach her to ride, but I figured today we could give her first lesson."

Claire pauses, turning to me. "Tyler, I don't know how to ride a horse."

"I figured as much, but that's why your lessons start now," I say, grabbing a cowboy hat from the rack placing it on her head before pulling her in, needing another taste.

I lean in, capturing her lips with mine, savoring the moment of peace that surrounds us as I enjoy her.

I accepted defeat last night. There is still so much she doesn't know, and it's all my fault. I have been so afraid that once she knows the hell I have caused, she won't want to see me again. I realize that's what I deserve. To suffer, to feel the pain that the ones I hurt have no choice but to live daily. For the first time, a selfish part of me is ripping through. Desperate to live, desperate to feel, and I will be damned if I want to shut it off.

Claire looks up at me through her lashes. Something written behind her eyes I can't read. I am sure it's questions, and I am going to answer every single one of them.

"Better head out of here before I change my mind and bring you back upstairs," I joke.

A laugh falls from her lips.

"Alright, let's go." She fake pouts.

"Let's go. I want to see that pretty ass on a horse," I tell her as we finally break apart and head out the door.

The stables are about a half mile down the ranch and since we are limited on time, I decided to drive it. Claire sits quietly, staring out the window, seeming to argue with herself.

"What are you thinking?"

She looks over at me, holding my eyes for a second before she looks down at the fingers that she's playing with in her lap.

"I don't want to overstep or anything. It's just that last night I realized you had quite a big scar and I was wondering what happened," she says to me.

I suck in a breath. I knew today it would all come out, but I was planning to wait until we got to the spot and then talk.

"You don't have to tell me, it's honestly none of my business. I just—" she rambles.

"Claire, it's okay," I tell her. "When I was eighteen, I had just graduated high school. A couple of my buddies had a party out in their parents' field. It was just supposed to be the seniors from the football team, but when I got there, there had to be over a hundred people." I pause, thinking back to that moment. A searing pain shooting through the deep scar etched across my stomach. "My mind had screamed to leave right then. Something inside of me knew that it wasn't a good idea, but I was the quarterback. Somehow, I had managed to become top of high school social circle and I was so high on everything going right, I stomped the warning into ash and walked right into that party like I owned it."

I park the truck and shut off the ignition, turning to Claire, who reaches out and grabs my hand. I almost feel guilty for taking it. She thinks I am the victim here when I'm really the villain.

"As soon as I walked over, people started handing me things. Shots, beers, weed. It didn't take long before I was on another planet. This wasn't a new thing for me, though. I spent most of my life after my dad died high or drunk."

I suck in a breath, the weight of that day so heavy I feel like it may suffocate me. I look back up at Claire, who is just looking at me with no judgment, waiting to see what I say next.

My thoughts are cut off by the sound of someone yelling in the distance. I look up to see a few of my guys running across the field.

Claire and I both shoot up and I jump from my side, with her following right behind me. Layton sees me and throws his arms in the air.

"Lightning is going crazy," he shouts across the field.

"Claire, I am so sorry. If you want, you go see Ohana, I have to deal with this horse. He's a pain in my ass," I say, quickly jumping from the truck, knowing if Layton is acting like that, it can't be good.

She smiles, undeterred that our day just got sidetracked and seemingly unbothered by everything I've told her so far. I try not to get my hopes up though, since she hasn't heard the best part of the story yet, where I ruin everything.

"This horse is a lost cause, man," Layton says as I walk up to him.

"If Granddad wasn't so insistent I keep him, I would have sold his ass months ago," I say on an annoyed breath as we all stand staring at him freaking out, unsure how to even begin to calm him.

"I honestly don't think there is anything left we can do. We've tried everything."

Lightning lifts, kicking his back legs into the air. His all-black coat shining in the sun. He is the most beautiful horse on this ranch, which is saying something since there are about fifty others, but he bleeds defiance.

Out of nowhere, his ears perk up. He seems completely calm as he trots towards us. Most of the guys run and jump the fence while Layton and I stare confused at each other by his sudden shift. We freeze as he approaches, then walks right between us towards the fence.

"Oh, wow," I hear Claire's voice behind me, causing Layton and my head to whip around. "I am sorry. The guy in the barn asked if I could step out for a second while he moved a couple of animals around.

The stubborn horse walks right up to her, stopping before leaning his head down. She reaches up, gently petting him, while every cowboy on the ranch stops and stares in wonder.

"Holy shit, you are dating a princess," Layton says, smacking my shoulder.

Claire must feel the shift because she awkwardly looks up at everyone gawking at her.

"He doesn't seem that bad to me," she says innocently.

One of the guys Lightning threw across the stables laughs.

"What are you, a horse whisperer?" he asks her.

"Well, seeing as this is the only horse I have ever seen, I don't know." She laughs. "Seriously, is he that crazy? You guys are acting like I am petting a lion or something."

"Oh, trust me, it's not that far off." Layton lifts his sleeve to a massive bruise. "That asshole bit me this morning."

Lightning lowers his head deeper toward Claire.

"Buddy, you can't bite Layton. He is our friend, okay? Plus, he fixed my car, so we owe him," she says to him in a baby voice.

My eyes shoot up to Layton.

"You fixed her car?" I ask him in shock.

He gives me a warning glare.

"Yeah, it was no big deal. It needed some spark plugs and a new part. She's as good as new."

"What the hell?" I mouth to him. The car needed a new engine. By the way Claire is acting, she didn't just drop new engine money, which means Layton lied about the part.

We are now in a silent battle. Thankfully, Claire is so wrapped up in petting Lightning, she doesn't realize it.

"I can't believe we thought it was dead," she gushes. "I can't thank you enough. I didn't even know you had it until Trish told me last night."

His eyes shoot to the ground. A look I know all too well from Layton. He is hiding something, which makes no sense because he never hides a girl from me. Normally, I'm begging him to not tell me the things he does.

I shoot him another questioning look and he just shakes his head at me.

"Claire, why don't we walk Lightning back to his stable? Then we can start your riding lesson. Hell, the way this just went, I am thinking it may be easier than I thought," I tell her, grabbing Lightning's reins and leading him toward the barn, my brain racing with questions.

Chapter Fifteen

Claire

Everyone stared as we walked back to the barn with Lightning, him happily trotting behind us without a care in the world. I felt bad locking him in the small stable, but Tyler assured me he's normally calmest in there.

I am now face to face with yet another horse named Lucy. She is the complete opposite of Lightning. Her soft white coat is marked with a few tan patches on her back and face. She approaches me easily, but no one gawks at the sight. Tyler told me she was his best starter horse. *Whatever that means*. So here I am, watching him throw a saddle over her back, contemplating all the choices I have made over the last few months to land me in this spot.

"You seem sweeter than Lightning, but I am somehow more afraid of you," I tell her quietly. "I guess it could be because I've gotta sit on you. Not that you don't look like a great horse to sit on or anything. It's just that I am from the city, and you don't really sit on horses in the city." I look up and see Tyler looking at me. His eyebrow arched as he tries to hold back a chuckle. He walks behind me, wrapping his arms around my waist.

"Well, she is all ready to sit on if you want to, but I will never force you to do anything you aren't comfortable with. So, if you don't want to ride today, you don't have to. I probably should have asked you before we got to this point, honestly."

"Oh, I want to," I say, looking at the size of the horse in front of me. "I am not going to lie though. These things are so much bigger than I thought they would be."

"I know they seem intimidating, but I promise you are in great hands with Lucy. I would never put you on a horse I didn't trust," he says, placing a kiss on the side of my neck before breaking away from my back and grabbing my hand. He pulls me in to face him, locking in on my eyes.

"Are you sure you want to do this?" he asks. "No pressure."

"I'm sure."

"Alright, let's get you up there," he says, walking me over to the saddle. "You are going to take your left foot and put it in here and grab her with your hand. Once you do that, use your body to throw your other leg over top of her. I will be right here to help you the entire time."

I follow his instructions, grabbing on to the saddle with one hand and placing my foot in the stirrup, then throwing my leg over and sitting before I have a chance to over think.

"That was perfect," Tyler says. "Are you comfortable?"

"I am honestly scared to death right now," I say, a slight shake of my words.

Concern instantly overtakes his smile.

"But I feel like such a badass I don't even care," I say excitedly.

Old Claire would never have done this. Old Claire wouldn't have lived. My mind flashes back to Michael. Us standing in my living room about a year ago fighting.

"You need to lighten up. One day when I am finally gone, I hope you get that chance. You spend every day so worried and locked in your head that you refuse to see you've wasted your entire life on me," he cried, his voice so broken it shot straight through me.

"Michael, don't say things like that. I love my life and I love you," I pleaded back to him.

"You will never get it because you got all the good you got from mom while I'm stuck like him. You don't know the hell it is knowing you are like that piece of shit," he argued back.

"You and dad are nothing alike, but you have yourself so convinced you're a monster that you refuse to see how much good is really inside of you," I told him, praying something will get through.

"One day you are going to live. I am going to move far away, and you are going to be forced to live your life for you for once, and that makes me the happiest brother in the world," he whispered, walking away, leaving me with tears streaking my eyes.

You were wrong, Michael. I think to myself. *I didn't need you to leave me, because you took a piece of me with you that will always be broken without you. I needed you to heal. I needed you to want to live. I needed you to fight for me as hard as I fought for you. I needed you and you left. And accepting that you felt that was your only choice is the hardest damn thing I have ever had to do.*

"Hey, you okay?" Tyler's voice breaks through my thoughts.

"Ya, I'm so sorry," I say, desperately wiping at the tears streaming down my face.

"You don't have to be sorry. If this is too much, you can get down," he says to me.

"No, this is amazing. I promise just got a little sidetracked is all. I have never done anything like this. It's intense," I tell him.

"Okay, well, you want me to start walking her?" he asks.

"Absolutely," I say excitedly, because I am riding a horse and Michael would be proud.

Even though I will never agree with his thought that I am better off without him, I know I can never change his mind. He is gone. He made my choice for me, so I will live the life he so desperately thought I deserved.

Tyler walks Lucy, and even though we are going beyond slow, I feel like I am on top of the world.

"What do you think?" Tyler asks.

"This just might be the best moment of my life," I say happily. "Can I go a little faster?"

"Yup, I am going to hand you the reins. Lucy won't go much over a trot these days, so no worries there. I am going to be right here the entire time. Just let her walk slowly. Use your feet right here to make her go faster and pull like this on the reins to stop her," he says, looking up at me like he has all the faith in the world.

It must rub off because I am feeling like I could ride a bull right now.

"Got it!" I gently tap Lucy's side with my feet, and she trots off around the circle fence line.

I can feel the laughter bubbling from inside of me as we trot circle after circle. Five circles in, Tyler must feel like I have it down pat because he hops on another horse, named Earl, and trots up alongside me.

"I can't say I am shocked you are a natural," Tyler says as he reaches me. "Are you ready to head out of the fence, or you still want to take a few more loops?"

"I am so ready." I pat Lucy lightly on the neck. "This may be my new favorite hobby."

"What was your old favorite hobby?" he asks.

"I don't think I had one," I tell him honestly at the realization before giving Lucy a light side tap and having her speed up toward the fence opening.

"Already a professional, I see," Tyler says with a laugh as he passes me.

I follow behind him, enjoying just how beautiful the ranch really is as the warm summer sun beats down on my back. The sun shines brightly over the green fields as cows graze in the pastures in the distance. Tyler keeps going until we are surrounded by fields filled with wildflowers that go so far in every direction it feels like they must never end. On the far side of the treeline, is a dirt road that stretches as far as the eye can see.

"Tyler, this is incredible."

"This isn't even the best part," he says before turning off the dirt road onto a path through the trees. I follow him down until the sound of water floats to my ears.

"Welcome to Magnolia Falls." I follow him through the opening to a beautiful waterfall surrounded by magnolia trees in full bloom mixed with the just start of fall leaves.

Tyler jumps from his horse, but I don't move. I am not sure if I could even get off on my own if I wanted to, but right now I'm frozen. I stare at the water gently crashing into the river below.

"This is…" I tell him my brain is unable to even come up with an adjective to describe the beauty before me.

"It really is, right? Getting to see the Magnolias this time of year is rare, but the warm front gave us a second bloom." Tyler says now alongside Lucy as he looks out at the view with the same amazement, even though I am sure he's seen it a million times. "It looks even better from the water."

Tyler helps me climb off Lucy, then walks her over to Earl, where he tethers her up so she can drink. The horse leans down, taking sips of water from the stream. The warm sun glistening off their coats.

"You coming in?" Tyler asks as he pulls his white t-shirt over his head. The view has just gotten substantially better. In the dark, Tyler's body is amazing, but here in the broad daylight as the sun highlighting every hard line, I cannot stop myself from staring.

I break my stare to throw my shirt over my head, tossing it behind me, uncaring of where it lands, and shimmy off my jean shorts alongside it. Tyler is already down to his boxers and jumping into the water. I run and jump behind him, the cool water sending a shock through my system. It feels fantastic after the heat beating onto my back from the ride.

Tyler swims up behind me, wrapping his arms around my waist.

"I really want to ask you if we are friends yet," he whispers in my ear. "But I am going to be honest with you, Claire. I am not sure if I want to be your friend anymore."

I suck in a breath as he pulls me even tighter against him.

"Tomorrow, I want to take you on an actual date. I want you to get all dressed up and I want to take you to dinner. Spoil you. Then I want to bring you home and rip off whatever sexy ass dress you have on and spend all night taking care of every inch of you," he says in my ear, his hand slowly tracing down the front of my bare stomach, sending butterflies to my core.

"Come with me," he says, releasing me and taking my hand, pulling me straight for the water that seems to be cascading from the sky. The cool mist falling over us.

"Ready?" he says over the steady sound of the water crashing in front of us. He pulls me through the soft flow into a small opening under the veil of water. Curtaining us from the world outside. Laying me on the cool smooth rock, he makes me feel as if I had become the waterfall surrounding us.

Chapter Sixteen

Tyler

I watch Claire and Mia running around the pen with Ohana, laughter floating through the air.

I feel happy. The guilt of that foreign feeling creeps into my brain, but I just as quickly shut it down. I will never forgive myself for what happened to Luke, but for the first time in years, I actually want to live again.

Like she can sense I am thinking about her, Claire looks back at me and smiles widely. Her blonde hair shimmering under the sun. I can't help the smile that breaks across my face.

"Well, if that isn't the face of a man in love, I don't know what is," Layton's voice says alongside me.

For a second, I think about denying it, but realize it's pointless. I know I'm falling in love with this girl.

"I don't know what I am doing. What if, when I tell her I am the reason for Luke's accident, she can't look at me the same?"

"You mean you and Luke's accident?" he says.

I shoot him a look because he knows I hate when he adds me to the story, like I suffered from that day the way Luke did.

"I think if she loves you half as much as I think you love her, she won't think a damn bit less of you, Tyler. One day, and I hope that day is standing right in front of us, you are going to realize nothing about that night was your fault. I hope like hell that day you finally forgive yourself."

I clench my jaw, biting back the words that want to escape. Anger at myself that Layton doesn't deserve to feel. He has always had my back, no matter what. Even when I haven't deserved it, he's always seen the best in me.

"So, you fixed the girl's car?" I ask, changing the subject.

He pauses, rubbing the scruff on his jaw. "Yeah, about that. I probably should have told you I did that. Trish asked about it, and I figured I would just see what I could do."

"So, you just casually put a new engine in an old hunk of junk because?" I ask him.

"Can you trust I had my reasons but can't exactly tell you them right now?" he asks me, his tone suddenly sad. I break my eyes off of the girls and look at Layton.

I hadn't realized, but he looks more stressed than I have ever seen him. Dark circles mar his usually bright eyes.

"You okay, man?"

"I'll be okay, just figuring some stuff out. It's been a little crazy, but it'll work out," he says.

"Hey, guys." Mia's voice breaks through our conversation.

Layton quickly throws on his worry-free smile like the entire conversation had been a figment of my imagination.

"Hey, I saw you riding earlier, Mia. Way to show all of them boys up out there," he says with a laugh, throwing his hand up for a high five, which Mia happily accepts.

"I know, right? I can't believe how easy Betty is to ride," she gushes.

"That was all you, girl. Trust me, I have seen a ton of people out here fail, especially at riding even with a calm horse like Betty." He laughs, causing Mia to smile from ear to ear. "Well, it's getting late. I better head out, gotta make a couple of stops before I go home."

"Thank you again, Layton," Claire shouts after him as he walks away.

"That's what friends are for. Glad I could help," he says, leaving us in the pink cast of the sunset.

"Can I put Ohana up?" Mia asks.

"I think Ohana would love that," I tell her. "Ask Derek to help you lock his gate. It gets tricky sometimes, okay?"

"I will!" she says as she skips away.

"I have never seen her as happy as she is today. She couldn't stop talking about your mom. She said she made her pancakes for breakfast, and they were the best thing she ever had in her life."

"My mom does make the best pancakes," I tell her as I watch Mia walk Ohana into the barn. Derek walks up to her, a big smile on his face.

"How old is Derek?" Claire asks.

"Just turned nineteen."

"That makes sense. I think he may have a slight crush." She laughs.

Mia pulls her phone out of her pocket before wrapping Derek in a hug. He turns the same bright he did while he stared at her swimming in the falls earlier today.

"Claire, can you drive me to Tyler's mom's? I want to talk to you about something," Mia says as she runs back over to us before she looks over her shoulder at Derek with a shy smile.

"Actually, that's probably a good idea. I should head home; I still need to do my laundry and notes for work tomorrow," she says, wrapping me in a hug and placing a chaste kiss on my lips.

She quickly pulls back, looking unsure about her choice. I loop my fingers through the loops on her pants, tugging her back into me before placing a deep kiss on her lips. She pulls away with flushed cheeks and a smile.

"Hey, Claire?"

"Hmm."

"Are we friends yet?" I whisper in her ear.

I hear Mia mumble, "That looks like way more than friends," under her breath, causing Claire to crack up laughing.

"I thought you said you didn't want to be friends, Tyler Henry."

"Does that mean you are saying yes to my date this Friday?"

"I think it does," she says with a smile.

I desperately try to peel my eyes open, but they feel super glued shut. I try to move, but I can't. Finally, I use every ounce of willpower I possess to break the invisible vise-grip on my eyelids.

The lights shine viciously, making me slam them back shut just as quickly as they opened.

"Why are the lights so bright?" I whine, my throat scratching and painful.

"Tyler!" I hear my mom say. "He's awake!" she shouts.

Confusion wraps around my brain. There are pieces of memories scattered across my mind, but nothing makes sense. I risk opening my eyes again against the burning light and this time I fight through the blurs of pain to try to piece together the sudden rush of chaos around me.

"Hi, Tyler, my name is Kathy. I am your nurse. I just paged your doctor. He will be here shortly," she says sweetly. Behind her, another three nurses shuffle through the door. The sound of the hand sanitizer dispenser echoes in my mind above all the voices and questions being asked around me.

"Sir, do you know where you are?" another nurse asks.

"I am assuming the hospital," I answer, confusion etched in my mind, but I feel the pieces gaining clarity.

"Did something happen at the party?"

"There was an accident; you were hit by a car," she replies.

She continues explaining something, but her voice is drowned out by the memories crashing into me.

I was with Luke, standing in the field, yelling at him for coming to the party.

A sound came out of nowhere. A car horn, but it didn't make sense. We were way off the dirt road, in the field. But it was too late to question.

I watched Luke turn towards the noise; a look of panic took over his face before a pain unlike anything I had ever felt burst through my side.

Then I was flying, darkness drowning out the screams. I desperately felt for Luke, my hands hitting the wet empty space around me. A metallic tang filling my mouth and nose as I struggled to suck in a breath through the thick liquid pouring out of me.

"Luke."

"Luke."

"Luke!" The black clouds tunnel my vision, my lungs burn until nothing is left.

"Tyler, no, I am so sorry. Don't die! No, please no." *The voice is so familiar but too far away to make it out.*

More screaming seemed to come from everywhere and nowhere at all. I felt the deep pain throughout my body disappearing as I welcomed the comfort of the darkness.

The ding from my phone breaks the fog.

Claire - I am so sorry, Tyler, but I have to cancel. I have an emergency meeting in twenty minutes. I would skip it, but I really can't. I may be stuck here for a while.

Tyler - That's okay. Rain check?

Claire - Please. I feel so bad. I was so excited to go.

Tyler - Don't feel bad. Life happens.

Tyler - When was the last time you ate?

Claire - I had a bagel at ten. I skipped lunch because I was excited about tonight. But I'll be fine until I get this handled.

I glance at the five on the clock and do a quick U-turn to the deli I just passed. *I will just grab her something quick she can eat before her meeting starts. I'm only five minutes away.*

Chapter Seventeen

Claire

I peek down at my last message to Tyler. I hope he isn't upset that I canceled. Knowing him, he was almost here when I texted him.

"Claire, I cannot thank you enough for doing this for me," Phillip says. "My nephew has struggled for a long time but has been clean for about a year. Him moving back here is challenging his resolve. This place brings back a lot of terrible memories for him, but that is his story to tell you."

"Anytime, Phillip, that's why I'm here," I tell him. The bell above the door dings, drawing both Phillip's and my attention. A large frame steps through the door with his eyes cast to the ground.

"Jake, glad you made it," Phillip says, walking up to place his hand on his shoulder. "Claire, this is my nephew, Jake. Jake, this is Claire."

"Hello, Jake, it is so nice to meet you," I say. He looks up with a deep sadness in his eyes that almost makes me step back. It is like I am looking into my brother's eyes all over again.

"Hey," he mumbles. "Sorry, I am a little early. I can wait if you need me too?"

"Well, alright I will leave you to it. Jake, if you want to come by after, I will have supper," Phillip says before walking out the front door, leaving me and Jake alone.

"Okay, I am not sure what Phillip has told you, but this is your safe space. You can open up as much or as little as you feel comfortable. I will give you some hopefully helpful tools to help you keep your recovery going," I tell him. He takes a deep breath, finally seeming ready to move to the next step when the bell dings again, causing us both to look over.

"Hey, I know you said you would be okay until after your meeting for dinner, but I figured I would drop something off just in case," Tyler says as he walks through the door. His eyes locked on me with a huge smile lighting up his face.

I smile back. A giddy feeling swimming throughout me. I have never had anyone care like Tyler.

"Oh, sorry man, I didn't realize you were already—" His words are harshly cut off. His smile twisting into a murderous scowl that I follow to Jake, who has lost all the color in his face.

"Um, Tyler, this is Jake, my client," I say to him, hoping to calm whatever this strange mood shift is. "Jake, this is Tyler."

"What the fuck are you doing here?" Tyler says with deathly calm.

Jake doesn't answer, just stares at him like he may be sick.

"He is my client, Tyler," I say, my confusion slowly morphing to anger at whatever this is.

"He has a voice, Claire. He can answer for himself," Tyler clips at me. "So, Jake, what brings you back to Gainseburg? Haven't destroyed enough people's lives?"

"Tyler," I say, anger threaded in my words, but his eyes remain locked on the other man.

"No, he's right, I shouldn't be here," he says. I go to defend him, but he cuts me off.

"Tyler, you have to understand."

A manic laugh falls from Tyler's mouth.

"Understand? How about this Jake? Screw you. You need to go back to whatever scum hole you crawled out of because no one wants you here. You're a piece of shit," he shouts.

Jake shoves past us both and out the door. I call after him, but he leaves too quickly. I run to grab my phone to text Phillip to find him with little explanation, ignoring the raging man still in the room.

"Get out," I say to him, rage burning behind my eyes.

"Claire, listen," he says, his voice breaking from the evil that it previously held.

"How dare you?" I seethe. "Who do you think you are, coming into my job and harassing one of my clients? I worked my ass off for this job. I care about these people, and it takes months to gain their trust. Then you storm in here like a raging lunatic and have the audacity to act the way you just did."

I walk into my office, Tyler running after me, but I slam the door in his face, quickly twisting the lock. I can't hold back the tears any longer as they spill down my face.

"Claire, please, I am so sorry. Let me explain," he begs.

"I need you to leave," I say, leaving no room for discussion.

"Claire."

"Tyler, get out now," I shout, a choked sob coming from deep within me.

Silence follows. It seems to drag for minutes until the soft sound of the bell dinging sounds through the door. I collapse to the floor, letting the sobs wrack my body.

"Sir, we need you to put down the weapon and put your hands up where we can see them so we can check on your wife," an officer's voice fills the silence.

"You think I give a shit about that bitch? That isn't my wife, at least not since she had them damn kids. They took my wife from me and left me with this shell of a woman. I can't stand another day of watching her live this way. She's already dead. You don't need to check. I made sure to finish the job," My dad says flatly.

The air whooshes from my lungs. I want to scream. I want to cry and never stop, but Michael is here, and Michael can't see me break.

"Sir, put the knife down now," the officer says again.

"You got any kids, officer?" my dad asks.

"Yes, I do," the officer replies. "I heard you have kids as well. You don't want them to lose their dad."

"I hate them goddamn kids. They ruined my life," he says again, like he isn't ripping the heart from my body. "I will make a deal with you, officer. How about I take both our kids' dads from them tonight?"

"He's charging."

Loud bangs rip through our house. I run, chucking my body over the top of Michael as he screams over and over.

His screams don't stop. Not after the bangs are long gone. His screams echoed over the officer's sobs that he had no choice. Not after the female officer comes to talk to us. Not after she leads us out, covering his eyes, while telling me to look the other way.

Not as I walk by the two white sheets stained red or the splatters of my father's blood painting our white living room wall. The deep red drips sliding down the family picture my mother insisted on hanging. His screams engraved their way so deep into me that even when I scrubbed myself that night with scalding water, they ate away at my brain.

I pull myself from the floor, trying to push the memories deep into my head again. It's been about an hour since Tyler left and, thankfully, Phillip texted that he found Jake and brought him home.

I lock up and head home. Pulling in next to Layton's truck. At this point, I have so many questions about him and Trish, but I am too damn exhausted to care.

I climb out of my car and walk to the steps where Layton is fixing our step.

"What are you doing here? I thought you had a hot date tonight?" he says with a laugh before looking up then jumping up to his feet. "What the hell happened?"

"Ask your friend," I tell him. "I don't know him at all apparently, since he likes to come into people's jobs and verbally assault their clients."

"Claire, that makes no sense. Tyler wouldn't do anything like that."

"I would have agreed with you about two hours ago, but I have never seen him like he was. He was scary."

"Who was it?" Layton asks.

"I can't really disclose my clients, Layton," I tell him as I pass by.

"I know that, but seriously, something isn't right. There has to be more going on," he says, concern written on his face.

I freeze, debating if I am willing to break the rules for a man that keeps breaking my heart.

"Was it Jake?"

My eyes fly up to his.

"Shit," he says, reaching into his pocket to grab his phone.

"Layton, what is going on?" I ask him. "Who is Jake?"

He rakes his hand through his hair, tugging at the ends.

"He is a bad part of Tyler's past. Probably the worst part. He's the real reason Luke is paralyzed. He also has been living on the west coast for the last ten years. I don't think anyone knew he was back," he says pacing back-and-forth, dialing Tyler again with no answer.

"Claire, listen, you have every right to be pissed at the way he acted tonight because I can only imagine it was far from pretty, but I really need to find him. The last time he ran into Jake, Tyler spiraled hard for weeks."

All the rage that I simmered on for hours today vanishes and is replaced with worry.

"I am going to go check the bar," Layton says.

"I'll go to his house."

"Give me your phone," he says. I hand him it and he types in his number, calling me. "If we find him, we can let the other one know, okay?"

I nod as I run to my car and head toward the ranch.

I feel like I get there in half the time I normally would. Tyler's truck is nowhere to be found, but I still get out and knock, just to be sure.

After that, I drive to the ranch and drive around the roads, asking if anyone on the property has seen him, but no one has.

Layton's name lights up my phone and I shift into park in front of my last stop, turning him on speaker.

"Hey, any luck?" I ask him.

"Yeah, I just pulled in. His truck is here. I am going to go in and talk to him," Layton says.

"Oh, thank God."

A knock on my window causes me to look up. Derek is standing by my car, distraught.

"Layton, hold on," I say as I open the door, jumping out.

"What's wrong?" I ask him.

"Mia and I went into Ohanas' pen earlier and we must not have shut it good enough. When we came back from our walk, the gate was open, and he was missing. I tried to tell Mia to wait for Tyler, but she took off and I don't know where she went."

"What is going on?" Layton shouts through the phone.

"Ohana got out and Mia went after him. Derek said he can't find either of them," I tell him, panic clawing at my throat. "I am going to go look for them. Tyler showed us the falls. Maybe she went there first."

"Claire, just hold on. I will go in and get Tyler and we can all look together. You don't know your way around the ranch," he says over the sound of his truck door slamming.

"I'm fine, I need to find her."

"Claire, stay with Derek. Derek, go tell the guys on the ranch to leave whatever work they have left for the day and start a search. You and Claire stay put until I get there. I will be there soon." Then he hangs up.

"I'm not waiting, Derek. We are wasting time. It is supposed to storm soon. You go get the guys. I will go check the falls and if she's not there, I will meet you back here."

"Claire, this isn't a good idea. Layton is right. You don't know your way around."

"I will be fine," I tell him before jumping in my car and taking off down the lane to the falls. Derek throwing his arms up in defeat in the cloud of dust behind me.

Chapter Eighteen

Tyler

"Another whiskey?" The bartender asks. All I have in me is a simple head nod.

He slides it over and takes the two empty glasses next to it. Five whiskeys later, Claire's face is still popping into my mind and the pure look of betrayal is there. I know I acted like an ass. I know she deserves an apology, and she deserves to never speak to me again. I know better, but Jake being back has my brain so messed up, I can't even think of what to say for her to even begin to forgive me.

Jake is back and my mind screams. How could he even think showing his face in this town was a good idea? I hate him. I hate what he took from Luke. I hate who he made me become. I hate that he fills me with so much goddamn hate.

"Pity party is over, let's go," Layton says from behind me. For the first time in my life, I want to punch him.

"Layton, it's not a good time. I have had a bad day and I really don't have the patience for you right now," I tell him, tilting the glass of whiskey and finishing it in one swig. The burn drowning at least some of my self-pity. "Another please," I say to the bartender.

"He's cut off," Layton says behind me.

I jump from my seat, twisting to face him. Rage sinking deep into my veins like I have never felt before towards him.

"What the hell is your problem, man?" I seethe under my breath getting right in his face.

"My problem is you are so busy drowning out your problems you have forgotten you have responsibilities. Have you even bothered to look at your phone?" he says in a voice that instantly breaks through my whiskey-soaked brain.

Layton isn't angry. He's scared. His phone pings with a text and he quickly reads it.

"We have to go. Now," he says, throwing a hundred-dollar bill on the counter and then dragging me behind him, leaving no room for argument.

I dig my feet into the ground beneath me.

"What is going on?"

"Mia is missing. I guess Ohana got out, and she went after him. Claire called me from the ranch. She went there to look for you. I told her to wait until we got back, but she apparently doesn't know how to listen because she left on her own to find Mia."

I instantly sober up, rushing ahead of Layton out the door. The sound of his boots against the hardwood follows me.

"Jump in my truck," he says.

He takes off as soon as my door slams shut. I look at the angry sky ahead.

"Let me have your phone so I can try to call her. Mine is in the truck." He shoves his phone at me, never taking his eyes off of the road.

I click her name, the phone ringing three times before her voice greets me.

"Layton, I will be fine." Her broken voice comes over the line as the service cuts in and out.

"Claire, it's Tyler." I hear her suck in a breath.

"Where are you? I'm at the—" The phone cuts out.

I quickly tap her name again.

"Hi, you've reached Claire. Leave me a message."

"I can't get a call out," I say, looking toward the angry black clouds darkening the sky.

"When was the last time you checked the weather?" I ask.

"About twenty minutes ago. It's not looking good. There is a big storm rolling in on the radar," he says, eyes glued to the road. "Hopefully, the rain holds off until we find them."

As the words leave his mouth, a rumble of thunder shakes the truck and droplets splatter the window.

"Fuck," I say, punching the dashboard.

"We will find them, Tyler," Layton says.

"Yeah, how hard can it be to find a eighteen-year-old, a woman with a dead phone, and a cow in one of the worst storms of the year?" I ask sarcastically.

He grumbles something that sounds an awful lot like 'screw you' as he quickly turns onto the dirt driveway of the ranch. As soon as he gets to the front of the barn, I see Derek pacing back and forth. I jump out before the truck fully stops.

"Any luck?" I ask him, already knowing the answer.

"No, the guys won't let me help look," he says, sounding just as frantic as I am. "I could help. I know Mia better than anyone else here."

"Okay, Derek, you go with Layton and lead him where you think Mia would be most likely to go." Layton looks over at me and nods his head, shockingly accepting that a nineteen-year-old will be in charge of him.

"Did Claire tell you where she was going to start looking?" I ask Derek.

"She said the falls, but I already sent some of the guys that way and she was gone," he tells me. "They found her car a little bit past the trail. But there are four trails that start in that area. There is no service, so they all brought walkies."

"Alright, Layton, I'm heading down to Claire's car and going from there. We will both grab walkies. If you find anything, let me know." I start running to the office across the yard with Layton and Derek behind me when a worker runs out, cutting off my path.

"Sir, these are our last two, they are fully charged, and all have been changed to channel five. The cops should be pulling in any minute. I am waiting here to lead them out to start searching as well."

I quickly grab both walkies from his hand, toss one at Layton and jump on the Gator.

My brain is still buzzing with whiskey that would normally keep me from driving anything, but right now my focus is only on finding the girls. I slam my foot on the gas, shooting mud out behind me and heading toward the trail. Layton and Derek take off the other way.

It takes me half the time it should to get to her car. A few men run up to me, the rain already having soaked through their clothes. Their flashlights barely make a dent in the thickness of the dark surrounding us.

"We have guys searching every trail here, but there is no sign yet of either of them. The rain has washed away any chance of possibly finding footprints from them or the steer."

"Alright, you guys keep looking. I am going to walk down a bit, see if anything catches my eye. If you find anything at all, call it in. We have to find them soon. The weather is just getting worse."

They take off, the dim of their lights disappearing into the trees.

For the first time since Luke was hurt, I feel fear. True fear coursing through me. The girls are all alone, God knows where on this huge ranch, and I honestly don't know how to find them.

"God, if you are still listening to me up there, I really could use you now. I know I keep messing shit up." I pause internally cursing myself. "See, I'm a disaster. I don't know how much good I have left in me, but Claire and Mia, they are good. So, God, if you still have any room left in your heart for helping me right now, I would appreciate it more than ever."

Just then, a streak of lightning illuminates the dirt road ahead. Something pink catches my eye a few hundred feet away, and I take off running.

Chapter Nineteen

Claire

It feels like I have been walking for an hour. The sky is now completely black. I only have the flashlight from my otherwise worthless cell phone. There is no trail, just thick thorns that cut deep into my skin with every step I push further following the trail of random objects Mia left behind. Thunder cracks overhead and the rain picks up. I know she has to be petrified out here all alone.

"Mia!" I shout for the hundredth time, my throat scratching with pain.

I should have turned back and gotten help when I found her hoodie, but I never imagined she would have gotten so far. My light catches another patch of color standing out amongst the green and brown of the trees.

A beaded bracelet hanging from a low branch.

"Mia! Can you hear me?" I scream as loud as my lungs can manage, fighting the tears threatening to spill from my eyes. "Please!" I shout.

A sound catches my attention so faint I question if my brain is simply playing tricks on me, but when I start to convince myself, that isn't the case, I hear it again.

I run towards the sound of Mia yelling, "Help!" growing louder with every step. My feet are moving so quickly in the dark I don't even see the drop off in front of me until it's too late. My body flies over the edge, sliding down the slick mud. I desperately grasp for anything, my hand wraps around something for a second but quickly loses grip. Something hard smacks into my side, shooting pain through my ribs before I smack the ground, knocking the wind from my lungs. The light from my phone shining down from a couple feet up the hill.

"Oh my God, Claire! Are you okay?" Mia's voice pushes my adrenaline enough to pull myself to sit.

She is at my side reaching out to help me.

"Do you think you can get up? I am so sorry, I tried to warn you, but I was too late," she says tears are spilling from her eyes.

"I'm okay," I tell her, accepting her help to stand and biting back my urge to wince in pain. "Did you fall down that hill too?" I ask her desperately trying to see her in the shadow cast by my light.

"No, I climbed down," she says. "I couldn't get back up, and the stream is completely blocking any other way out."

She steps over, grabbing my phone from the hillside and shines it on a white and black ball of fluff standing eating grass like it's any other day.

"He doesn't seem hurt," she says, smiling.

I walk over to him, softly patting his head.

"You are trouble, buddy," I tell him softly. "I'm glad you are both okay, though."

I stand back, taking in the steepness of the hill. It is about ten feet to the top, but basically a ninety-degree climb. The thunder booms so loudly I swear I feel the ground shaking beneath us, it's almost instantly followed by another bright streak of lightning breaking through the darkness of the trees.

"Claire, I'm scared," Mia cries alongside me. "I think the stream is getting higher."

"What do you mean it's getting higher?" I ask her, looking back at the rushing water about twenty feet from touching the side of the steep wall of dirt.

"When I first got down here, that big rock was on the edge of the stream and now it's almost covered with water." I shine my light to where she's pointing. A large rock is sticking out a couple inches about two feet off of shore.

I look back in front of me, realizing how bad this situation really is.

"I am going to try to climb up. When I get to the top, I can pull you out," I tell her, trying my best to hide my fear. I am not optimistic in my ability to get back to the top and my body is already screaming from the previous fall.

"What about Ohana?" Mia asks. "How can we get him out?"

"Mia, we are going to have to go find Layton or Tyler to get him. There is no way we can do it ourselves." I see her face sink in the cast of the flashlight.

"What if we aren't fast enough?" she asks me.

"Don't think that. We can do this."

I grab onto a branch sticking from the side of the wall and begin to pull myself up, my feet slipping in the muddy side of the hill. I get up a few feet before I lose traction all together and slide back down, hitting my already sore ribs against the rough dirt and rocks. I feel a tear spill down my cheek, but quickly wipe it away.

"I should have chosen better shoes for mountain climbing," I say, forcing a laugh as I begin to climb up again my flats losing tractions and slipping out beneath me once again. This time I lose my grip completely, landing hard on my butt.

"Come on!" I shout to the sky.

"Boost me up," Mia says. The fear in her voice is gone.

"Mia, no you could get hurt. It's so slippery and there are rocks." I could never forgive myself if she fell.

"I know we need to get out of here quickly." She shines the light over to the rock now, only a sliver of it showing above the surface of the brisk moving water. The shore is even smaller than it was a couple of minutes ago. "We are out of time, so boost me up! If I can grab on to that root, I can pull myself to where the hill gets less steep and get up. Then I can pull you up."

I know she's right; if we stay here, we are going to end up swept up in the stream. I look at Ohana. He stopped eating and is now curled in a ball pushed against the side of the hill, shivering. My eyes fill with tears because I don't think he is making it out of this.

"Okay," I tell her. "I will lean my back against the hill. Put your one foot in my hands and I will boost you up so you can step on my shoulders. Hopefully that's enough."

"Okay," she says, coming forward quickly wrapping her arms around me. "We are getting out of here, Claire."

I smile at her confidence, trying my best to believe her, and weave my fingers together. The hard rubber of her sneaker digs painfully into my palm as she hoists herself up my body. Her chest smacks into my face pushing my back painfully into the dirt behind me, but I ignore it.

"I'm so sorry!" she shouts down at me, her head now above mine.

"Don't be sorry. On the count of three, I am going to shove you up. Step on my shoulders, okay?" I say, my voice shaking against the pain tearing through my body.

"One, Two, Three."

I use every ounce of strength in my body to shove her up. Her one foot comes down onto my left shoulder, digging in. Her right foot leaves my hands and quickly lands on my other shoulder. My body screams at me to fall, but I lock my knees. The rain pouring down around me drowns out the sound of everything else. Suddenly, the weight leaves me. I turn around, trying my best to look up to Mia, the rain blurring most of the light from reaching her.

She is almost to the top, her hands wrapped tightly around the twists of the roots shooting out of the thick brown dirt. She pulls one foot up, securing it on a rock before pulling herself up even closer to escape. Her arm reaches up higher grabbing another piece of the root and her foot follows to yet another rock.

"You got it, Mia! You're so close!" I shout up to her. Her chest hits the crest of the hill when her foot slips. My breath leaves my lungs as I watch her dangle from the edge. She manages to lock her foot on the edge of the roots and pull herself the last bit before jumping to her feet.

"Oh my God, I did it!" she shouts down happily. "Come on, Claire."

"Go, Mia. I will be fine, just go get help," I yell at her.

"I can't leave you here, the water is rising," she cries down. I can feel her panic creeping in. I quickly toss my phone as hard as I can towards her, thankful it lands over the ledge. "Claire, please just let me try!" she begs.

"I can't, Mia, if you fall you could get hurt and then we will never get out of here. So go! Follow the trail you left and bring back help. We will be okay, I promise." She hesitates for a minute.

"I will be right back, I promise you. I love you." Then she takes off, taking the light with her. The darkness that is left is unlike anything I have ever been in. I feel the panic start to crawl up my throat, ripping the air from my lungs. I slide down the muddy wall, sitting on the ground as shivers wrack my body before a warm mass cuddles up alongside me. Ohana putting his wet, oversized head in my lap. I softly pet him, feeling the panic slowly break.

"We are going to be okay, buddy, I promise. They are coming back for us." I wrap my arms tightly around him, hoping that I am telling the truth.

Chapter Twenty

Tyler

"I found Mia's hoodie. Send a few guys to meet me on the road about a hundred yards past Claire's car," I call over the walkie talkie. "Some of you stay behind just in case it's a dead lead."

I want to go, but I know having other men looking will better our chances of finding them. The minutes drag on and still no one has gotten to me. My frustration boils over. The rain hasn't let up, and they have been missing for hours.

"I'm going by myself," I say over the walkie. "Find the hoodie and go from there."

My walkie blows up after that, but I am already on my way into the thick of the woods. I start to question if I made the right choice since there is no trail to follow, but my light catches a hat hanging from a tree branch ahead.

"Claire, Mia!" I yell, but it's met with nothing but the growl of angry thunder and the pounding of rain.

I walk to the hat and shine my spotlight around, seeing something else leaning against a tree ahead. Thank God they thought to mark their way. I am almost to the tree when a flash of light ahead of me catches my attention from deep within the woods.

"Claire?" I shout. No response. "Mia, is that you?" The light keeps moving forward, coming in and out of focus. I start to run towards it, screaming the girls' names over and over as I go.

"Tyler!" I hear the faint yell from Mia in the distance.

I pick up my speed, running way too quickly through the thick brush, letting my skin rip against the briars without care. Finally, I see Mia's small frame in my light. I shine it around her, but she's alone.

My heart sinks.

"Mia, are you hurt?" I yell as I reach her. Trying my best to look over her. Her hair is caked with mud that drips down her face into her eyes.

Her lips are light blue and trembling uncontrollably, but she seems okay.

"I'm fine. You need to get Claire," she says, her voice cracking. "She made me leave her all alone out there. I didn't want to, but I had to."

I grab my walkie talkie.

"How far out are you guys from the hoodie? I have Mia. I need to go get Claire."

"We just entered the woods by the hoodie." I see their light shining behind us as the response comes through.

"She's still out there, Tyler! You have to hurry. The river is flooding, and they are stuck," Mia says. Her breathing is getting quicker. I can tell she is on the verge of a panic attack.

"Where is she?" I ask.

Mia looks at me, her face etched with fear, her breathing now erratic.

"Mia, please! I know you're scared, but you need to tell me where she is and who is with her so I can help her."

"I left a trail. There are about four more things and then there is a drop off. The ledge is too steep to climb, and the river is rising on the other side quickly. Claire is down there with Ohana, and I think she may be hurt from falling," Mia blurts out quickly, just as two of my guys reach us.

The air rushes from my lungs. I lock eyes with the guys.

"Get her to safety and get her warm. Send everyone my way with ropes, blankets and whatever else they can grab to help me. Tell them to follow the trail of stuff and to meet me there." I turn and run towards the next object before anyone has the chance to respond.

I am not letting her down. I refuse to lose her. I know I am running as fast as I can through the thick twisted brush, but I feel like I am moving in slow motion, desperately begging my body to push harder to no avail as I see a bracelet hanging from a branch ahead.

"Claire!" I yell, knowing I will be met with more silence.

I push deeper, another flash of silver catching my eye, and I run to it. A necklace dangling loosely from a branch. It should be here, but I desperately look around and see no sign of a drop off—and no sign of Claire.

"Claire, please! Where are you?" My voice cracks with frustration and defeat. I look around again, praying to find another breadcrumb to follow. I drop to my knees, the rain finally letting up some and allowing the quiet to surround me. Everything is silent save for the sound of rushing water to one side. I turn again, shining my light towards the sound, realizing in the distance the tree line simply disappears. Which would only make sense if it dropped off there. I run towards it. The angry roar grows so loud it's almost deafening.

The edge comes into sight. I scream Claire's name again, scared to death to look over the side and find that she's not there. Still, I can't hear anything over the water.

I drop to my stomach, climbing towards the steep edge through the cold wet mud until I can peek over the edge. Shining my light. The roaring water flowing against the side of the drop and no sign of anyone else being there.

"No!" I scream into the darkness. "God, no. Please, no."

I shine my light desperately in every direction over the ledge when I catch the smallest flash of white in the distance. I roll back and jump to my feet, running towards it, bile rising in my throat at the thought that I am most likely too late. It's obvious she got caught in the current. I get to where I can look over, dropping back down the pain of the sticks and rocks digging into my chest, barely registering. I climb to the edge and shine my light down, catching on the white and black fur of Ohana. He is laying on a small piece of dry land, his back end already getting overcome with the current. His body protectively pinning something against the wall of the drop off.

"Claire!" I shout, realizing she isn't moving. Ohana barely reacts, just a soft huff, almost like he is so thankful to hear my voice, but he doesn't move from holding her.

I quickly look around, trying to figure out the safest way for me to get down when a light shines from behind me.

"Tyler!" Layton shouts. I jump from the ground, shining my light his way.

"Hurry, I found her. I need help!" He is at my side with three other men not far behind. "I need a rope. She's down there."

He tosses it at me before dropping to his stomach to assess the situation.

"Shit," I hear him say under his breath. "Claire, hang tight for us. Tyler is coming to get you."

Neither of us even know if she's alive to hear him, but I am glad that he is reassuring us both. Once I have the rope tied around me, I toss the opposite end to Layton and start to climb down.

"Layton, I won't be okay if she's not okay," I tell him, taking a second to swallow the fear in my throat. He simply nods, his eyes etched with sympathy.

I know he wants to reassure me, but he knows as well as I do how bad this is. I drop over the side, not wasting another second. My feet hit the soft ground, my boots sinking into the soft flooded ground. I run to her side, dropping down. Ohana softly peeks up at me and I see how tired he is.

"It's okay, buddy, you did good. I need to see her now, okay," I tell him, softly patting his head before he moves it off her, still not bothering to get up or leave her side.

She's pale. I check her pulse and feel the relief flood in when I feel a faint flicker against my fingers. My adrenaline kicks in. Time to get her the hell out of here.

"She's alive!" I shout up to the guys. "I am going to try and hold her and climb at the same time. When I say 'ready', pull."

I softly pick her up. "I got you, baby," I whisper to her as I gently put her over my shoulder, holding her limp body tightly with my one arm while using the other to grab on to a branch. I glance back at Ohana, who is still laying in the same spot, the water rising quickly. "Hold on, buddy, we will be right back for you, okay," I tell him before yelling up to the guys to pull us up. My heart breaks the higher I get from him as I watch the water overtake his weak body.

As soon as we hit the top, I lay Claire on the ground and quickly untie myself.

"Someone go get the steer!" I shout, dropping to my knees, feeling again for a pulse.

Nothing. I hold my breath and I start compressions.

"Come on, baby, come back to me. I can't lose you, Claire Elizabeth. I love you."

I cry to her, desperately pumping her chest in the dark. I breathe into her mouth.

Nothing. "Claire, please!" I say, starting compressions again.

Everyone around me watches in silence. Tears stream down my cheeks as pain tears through me. It feels like every bone in my body is splintering apart, exploding into pieces as I watch her lay lifelessly below me, her ribs cracking under the pressure of me pressing on her chest. My mind screams that she's gone, but I can't stop myself from repeating, my arms sinking down, desperate to restart her heart. I feel the vomit climbing up my throat. My brain shutting down as the blackness surrounding me, closing in and dragging me under. I won't stop, though. I keep pushing.

A cough rips from her mouth, water flying out towards me. I quickly grab her, rolling her on her side on auto pilot. She continues to cough, and people start dropping next to me, trying to help anyway they can. Finally, the coughing stops. She puts her elbow under her, trying to push herself up. I gently help her sit and climb in front of her, so her tear-stained face is resting in the palms of my hands.

I look her over. Taking in the panicked look on her face running my thumb over a small scratch on her cheek.

"Michael?" she says deliriously.

"Claire?" I ask. Still unable to believe she is okay. "It's Tyler." She pauses, glancing around at the group of people.

"I'm okay," she whispers, her voice scratchy as she winces.

I can't stop myself. I wrap her in my arms, tucking her head tightly under my chin, covering the top of her head in soft kisses and tears.

"I thought I lost you," I say, afraid to let her go.

Chapter Twenty-One

Tyler

I softly close the door to the spare room where Claire, Mia, and Trish are all curled up in bed. By the time I got Claire home, it was after two in the afternoon. When I walked out, they were already drifting off. I ran around the ranch trying to keep my mind busy, even though all the guys kept telling me to go in and rest. Now the sun is setting in the distance, and I am thanking God they are all still peacefully asleep.

"How are they?" Layton asks as I walk out of the door. He leans against the back of his truck, a sandwich in each hand. He passes one to me, looking just as disheveled as I am. The guys all told us to take the day off, but they were out looking for hours, too.

"They are all still asleep, thank God," I tell him, walking over to the truck next to Layton to lean against it with him.

We both stare in silence as the sun sinks and disappears in the distance. The exhaustion from not getting any sleep finally hitting me. I take the sandwich from his hand, taking a bite.

"Four broken ribs… I broke four of her ribs," I say, unable to hide the choke in my voice.

"You did what you had to do to save her life, Tyler," he replies, his back still pushed against the truck. "I am sure she'd much rather have a couple broken ribs than be gone."

"Yeah," I say softly, but it doesn't ease my guilt. "Any word from the vet on Ohana?" I ask him, desperate to change the conversation.

"I just got off the phone with him before you walked out here. It's not good man. He's showing signs of pneumonia. The vet is recommending stopping treatments. He said the costs to continue care are astronomical and we all know the odds of him coming out of this are virtually impossible," he says.

"Call him back and tell him to keep going. I need him to figure it out and save him," I tell Layton, pulling myself away from the truck to face him.

"Tyler, the bill could end up being tens of thousands of dollars, and more than likely he still won't survive." He huffs at me. "We both know how much of a hole that would put you in. I know you don't want to hurt the girls anymore, but you need to be realistic. We work around cattle every day. They don't survive shit like this."

"Are you going to go into that room and tell those girls that the steer that they believe saved Claire's life died because I didn't want to spend the money, Layton? Because I sure as hell am not," I bite out, "I don't care what it costs. I don't care if I am in debt for the rest of my life. If that steer dies, it won't be because I didn't try to save him."

Layton looks like he is going to argue, but instead he just softly shakes his head before grabbing his phone and walking away. I hear him tell the vet to keep going and keep us updated. I know he's right. The odds of him pulling through are damn near impossible, but I can't seem to accept it.

I stand there, leaning against the truck, staring in the distance until the guys clear out. No one stops to talk to me. They just offer sad smiles and half-assed waves as they walk by. I walk to the porch, sinking down into the old wicker chair and dropping my head into my hands.

"Hey," Claire says from behind me. "Everything okay?"

I turn towards her, the stress eating at me seems to melt away. She is still in my white t-shirt and sweatpants that are both entirely too big. I can't help but smile at how small they make her seem.

"I'm okay," I tell her.

She pauses studying my face.

"It's Ohana, isn't it?" she asks.

I don't want to tell her. She just went through enough, but I also need to stop hiding things from her.

"It looks like Ohana may have pneumonia," I tell her. "I told the vet to do whatever it takes. But honestly, if he does, his chances aren't good."

Her face drops.

"Do you think he's going to make it?" she asks, her voice just above a whisper, her eyes locked on me.

"I think if there is ever a steer to pull through, it's going to be him," I tell her honestly.

She gives me a sad smile.

"If he doesn't, it's going to break Mia," she says looking out to the starry sky.

"I know," I say, pointing to the empty spot next to me. "Why don't you come sit down? How are you feeling? You probably shouldn't be up."

She walks over, sinking down, and laying her head against my chest. I place my head on top of hers and softly rub circles on her shoulder.

"I am so sorry, Claire. For everything."

"It's okay," she reassures me, pulling back to look into my eyes.

"It's not okay, I acted like a child. I made a scene at your job. I went to the bar instead of fixing my mess, and you and Mia needed me. I owe you an explanation."

I put my hand on her face, running my thumb across her cheek, her blue eyes are on mine.

"I thought I lost you last night and I realize it was because I wasn't honest with you from the start," I say, pain lacing my words. "I spent so much of my life not caring about anyone. I felt like I didn't deserve to find that happiness because I stole it from Luke." Her eyebrows scrunch in confusion.

"I was the reason Luke went to that party. He was the perfect child, Claire, I was a disaster. I had just graduated. Our dad had passed away my sophomore year from a sudden heart attack, and I was mad at everyone because of it. I had a great life and a great family, but none of it seemed to matter. I had a scholarship for football at Arizona state. I was completely packed. I couldn't wait to go." I pause, taking a second to breathe.

"I went to a party at my friends. It was in the middle of a field. My last hoorah before I left. I remember sitting there, drunk and stoned, by the fire when I saw Luke pop out of the woods.

"I was pissed. I was so worried he'd see how messed up I was and go back and tell mom. We got into a huge fight. I had moved us far enough away that the party wouldn't hear us screaming at each other over the music. It was so dark I could barely see him in front of me. He told me that I had made mom suffer even more after losing dad than she deserved. Those words destroyed me because I knew he was right. That was the last thing I remember before waking up in a hospital room three days later. My mom was there when I woke up. She told me that we had been hit by a car. A group of my friends apparently went to stock up on beer. They were all drunk and thought it would be easier to just drive back in the field instead of carrying the beer back."

"And I am guessing Jake was one of those guys?" she asks me.

"He was driving. When my mom told me Luke was paralyzed, I prayed over and over that God would just kill me right then. I should have been the one that never walked again."

"The scars on your stomach?" she asks.

"I had a ruptured spleen, and a broken arm. The irony is that being drunk and high saved me. That was nothing. I was back to my life after a few months. Luke had to go through physical therapy for years. Now he's stuck in that chair. I ruined his life."

"Tyler, Luke is amazing. It seems like he's kicking ass, if I do say so myself," she says, grabbing my hands in hers. "You guys were all teenagers, doing stupid teenager things. Maybe you shouldn't have gone to the party. Maybe you should have handled losing your dad better. There will always be maybes, but you were a kid struggling through one of the hardest things a child can go through."

"I should have been there for them, Claire. Instead, I pushed them away and it cost my brother his normal life," I say.

"There is no perfect way to handle grief, Tyler. When I was twelve, my dad murdered my mom and was killed by the police. My brother and I heard it all happen. He was only nine. After that, we got shuffled around between family and foster care. I didn't speak a word for an entire year. Michael spiraled and became addicted to anything he could get his hands on. I came here because it finally became too much for him and he committed suicide," she says, with tears welling in her eyes. I suck in a breath and pull her into me. "We both lost them, and we both handled it the best we thought we could. I miss him every day, and I wish like hell he never touched all of those drugs, but I don't blame him. He was a child dealing with a pain he couldn't hold."

She pauses. I can feel her warm tears soaking through my t-shirt.

"You have spent all of these years blaming yourself, and I get that. I spent years asking myself why I didn't call for help sooner that night. Why I didn't tell someone before that night my dad had been abusing my mom. I blamed myself for Michael's addictions, but in reality, there was only so much I could control," she tells me.

I let her words sink in. It seems crazy that she would blame herself for her dad killing her mom. She was only a kid and I realize exactly why she's telling me this story.

"Claire, I am so sorry you had to go through any of that," I tell her, still holding her against my chest. She pushes back slightly.

"Me too, but the past is exactly that. The past. I can't go back and save my mom or my brother, and you can't go back and not go to that party. We can live now though," she says.

"It feels wrong that I get to live a normal life when Luke can't."

"Tyler, Luke is smart and driven. He is living and his only wish is that you start living too," she says, and my gaze shoots up to meet hers.

"Did he tell you that?" I ask her.

"Yup, the first night I met him," she says quietly. "He told me you gave everything for him, and he wanted to see you finally do something for you."

"I don't know how." And that's the truth.

"I think part of being able to move forward is healing all the parts of your past."

"How do I even begin to do that though?" I ask.

"Well, you seem to have a lot of anger towards Jake," she says, glancing down at her hands.

"I can't do that." I swallow back the anger that starts to bubble up in the pit of my gut.

"I get that," she says. "After my parents died, I was so angry. When we went into the system, they put us both in therapy. The therapist told me the best way to move on with my future was to forgive my past and everyone in it. Not for them, but for myself. I told her there was no way I could ever do that. Before I moved here, I stopped at my dad's grave. At first, I was full of rage. Then I told myself he was only human. A heartbroken man who watched the love of his life wither away with depression after having children and using addiction to cope. The drugs and alcohol are what turned him into a monster. What my dad did will never be okay. He stole my whole world from me, but I have made a million choices in my life that could have led me to ruin my life too, and I thank God every day that none of them did."

I take in what she is saying to me. I know Jake would have never intentionally hurt us, but the thought of looking at his face ever again pisses me off.

"I know you're right. I will think about it, but I can't make any promises."

She smiles, leaning her head back against my chest. "That's enough for me," she says.

I run my fingers softly through her hair until her breath evens out.

"I don't deserve you, Claire, but I will work my ass off trying too," I whisper before gently scooping her up and carrying her to my bed, crawling in alongside her and letting sleep drag me under.

Chapter Twenty-Two

Claire

"Has he called yet?" Mia asks as she jumps from Tyler's mom's car.

The sun paints the sky bright pinks and oranges on the horizon as it rises in the distance. Tyler's mom comes from her side and walks toward us. I wrap my sweater a little tighter against the chill of the Fall morning air as I stand to meet them at the front step.

"I'm sorry, Mia, no updates yet," I tell her. "Why don't you guys come in for some coffee? Tyler left some omelets for us that are still warm.

"Did you just say 'Tyler' and 'omelets' in the same sentence? Because I think I may have the wrong son," Pam laughs.

"He's been putting those cookbooks to work. They are actually really good too."

"I'm sorry I woke you up, Claire," Mia says as we walk through the front door. "You should be resting. You are probably in a lot of pain."

"You didn't wake me. I slept all day yesterday. I was wide awake before Tyler this morning. Plus, I am a lot tougher than I look."

Pam locks on me for a second, trying to read if I am lying about being in pain. Unfortunately, I have had a ton of practice pretending pain doesn't actually hurt. I just shoot her a reassuring smile. It does the trick. She walks over to the pot of coffee and starts making a cup.

"Ohana has to be okay," Mia says. "He saved your life."

"I know it doesn't look good, Mia, but like Tyler said. If any steer can survive, it will be Ohana," I say.

"I hope so," she replies solemnly as the sound of the front door opening fills the room.

"It's me," Trish says, walking into the kitchen and to my side. "Layton is on the phone with the vet," she says quietly.

"Layton?" I ask her under my breath, peeking over to Mia and Tyler's mom who are deep in conversation about hero cows.

"It's nothing, he just drove me here," she says. I want to argue that it makes no sense for him to drive her here when she drove my car home last night, but I bite my tongue.

"Do you know anything?" I ask.

"No, I think he was worried it wouldn't be good, so he told me to leave and then started whispering. How are you feeling? I figured you'd still be resting, but I guess I should have known better."

"I feel fine," I tell her.

"Claire, you may be able to trick a lot of people with that bull crap, but you can't trick me."

I glance back over at Pam and Mia. Mia is still talking like crazy, but Pam glances up at me, looking concerned. I smile again, hoping it's convincing, but she just looks back at Mia.

"Fine, it hurts like crazy," I tell her. "I know Tyler feels like crap, though. He keeps apologizing over and over like he didn't literally save my life."

"I get that. I just want you to take care of yourself, Claire. I almost lost you and I don't know what I would do with myself if that happened. You are my best friend in the entire world."

The sound of the door opening again makes all four of us look over to see Tyler and Layton enter.

"That was the vet; Ohana is looking way better. He said he has never seen anything like it. He didn't think he would make it through the night. Then this morning he was up walking around. His lungs are clear. He still needs to take it easy for the next week or so, but he sees no reason we can't bring him home," Tyler says, locking eyes on me across the kitchen.

I can't help the smile that overtakes me.

"I knew it!" Mia yells jumping from her chair, almost causing it to tumble over. "I knew he would be okay."

She runs to Tyler's side, wrapping him in an enormous hug.

"Layton is going to go pick him up. Would you and Trish like to go with him?" he says to Mia. "I think Layton could use some people with some heart to help him."

"Pam, can I?" she asks.

"Absolutely, you can," Pam tells her.

"Tyler, thank you so much for not giving up on him," she says before running towards the front door.

"I guess that is our cue to go," Layton says, looking at Trish.

"Sounds good to me," Trish replies. "We'll be back."

"I am going to head home for a little bit too. Mia was in such a rush, I didn't get a chance to give Goose his breakfast," Pam says, getting up and heading towards the front door.

"How are you feeling?" Tyler asks, coming up alongside me.

"I'm good."

"How are you actually feeling, Claire?" he asks leaning in closer to me, caging me against the counter.

"What is it with you all today? I'm fine," I say on a huff.

Tyler scrunches his eyebrows.

"Fine, I hurt," I tell him. "But please don't apologize again. You saved my life."

"Okay," he says, leaning forward and placing a soft kiss on my head. "I will try to stop apologizing. I don't know what you are doing to me, Claire. A few months ago, I would have been just like Layton, saying Ohana had no hope in hell because that is what made sense, but the thought of hurting you anymore made me sick. I never want to be the reason you are in pain again."

"I don't expect you to never hurt me again, Tyler. We will both keep messing up every day for the rest of our lives."

"I want to try my best to give you everything you deserve. I want to be a better me for you. I have no idea how it happened. Before you, I was fine being alone. Then somehow, in the last three months, you've destroyed every wall I built. I can't imagine a second without you. Seeing you laying there. Thinking I lost you before we ever even had a chance. I never want to feel like that again. I'm in love with you, Claire Elizabeth," he says.

"I'm in love with you too," I tell him. "I think I knew it all the way back when we met at the bar, and you sat outside with me. There was something about you that was unlike anyone I had ever met. Coming to this ranch, seeing you with your brother and Mia. You proved over and over again that I was right. I just never thought I could feel this way so quickly. It scares me."

His fingers brush across my cheek, making me look up at him. His green eyes locking onto mine.

"It scares me too, but not more than the thought of never having you. I've spent my whole life telling myself I don't deserve love. Then I met you and I have never needed something more. If you want to jump, I will jump in with you, and never look back."

"I have never wanted to jump more in my life than I do with you." I say, tears threatening to spill from my eyes.

He leans in, capturing my lips against his, and the world disappears. I am lost in him. His taste, his touch. I am free.

"He's home!" Mia's voice echoes through the house.

I jump from the couch, rushing to Tyler, who is making lunch in the kitchen.

"Let's go welcome our hero," he says, leading me out the door.

I look in front of me to see Ohana slowly walking in the field. It's obvious he is weak, but he is alive, and that's all that matters. Mia and Derek stand shoulder to shoulder, smiles plastered on their faces as they talk excitedly.

Layton and Trish stand next to each other far enough apart that they think it's not suspicious, but the way they keep glancing at each other makes it anything but. Pam smiles, taking everything in, and Tyler holds me like he may just never let me go again.

They all say when they looked down at the edge of the drop they saw Ohana on the side of the river protecting me. I remember, though. Michael dragging me to the edge. Pinning me to the side as the water rushed across his back, telling me over and over again that I was going to be okay. That it was finally his turn to protect me. His eyes clear, a smile lighting up his face. He looked free.

For the first time, his memory doesn't drown me. I realize forgiving him for setting himself free doesn't mean I wouldn't give the world to have him back. I know I will never agree that he wasn't worthy of every ounce of myself I poured out. I would choose him over me time and time again. And I feel like the best way I know how to do that now is healing. Letting go of the pain that controlled me for so long. Holding on to these new friends who have quickly become my family. To this man who loves me. To this town that has become my home.

I know I am going to be okay.

The End

Epilogue

Claire

One Year Later

"Tyler?" I call, walking into the kitchen putting the bag of groceries on our counter.

Charlie purrs and rubs against my legs, and I lean down to pick him up and run my hands through this soft black fur.

"Where is your dad?" I ask him as I tickle under his chin, feeling something there. I grab it pulling a piece of paper off his collar that has the word *backyard* written on it. I walk to the back door and throw it open.

"Surprise!"

The backyard is full of people smiling at me.

"Guys, it's not my birthday," I say, confusion lacing my words.

"We know that," Phillip says from across the yard. His granddaughter is wrapped tightly in his arms and daughter is next to him. "This is to celebrate you opening your own center."

I walk into the crowd of people in the yard. Trish runs up wrapping her arms tightly around me.

"I knew you were destined for greatness," she says, a huge smile across her face as she wraps me in a hug. "I'm so proud of you."

Layton walks up alongside her.

"I knew it the day Lightning walked up to you. Then you went and rode him, and now I'm convinced you are capable of anything."

"All of these people came for me?" I ask, shocked.

"Of course, they did," a voice says from behind me. I turn to Phillip. "You changed all of our lives, Claire. You gave me my family back."

"You did that all by yourself," I tell him.

"You keep telling yourself that," he says. Looking over to his daughter who is smiling at him, her little girl running across the grass laughing, her dark hair blowing in the breeze. "Honestly, I can never thank you enough for giving me the courage to keep fighting. For giving me a purpose."

"You have no idea how happy it makes me to see you guys together."

"I better get back over there," he says, putting a hand on my shoulder. "Don't think for a second that you don't deserve all of this."

With that, he walks away, leaving me to take in the crowd. Mia and Pam are at a table. Derek is across from Mia, not taking his eyes off of her as she talks to Pam. She leaves in a few weeks for veterinary school. I couldn't be more proud.

Jake and Luke are next to each other, laughing. Something I never thought I'd see. After everything that happened last year, Tyler decided to try and talk it out. The first few minutes dragged as they stared at each other in silence. Phillip and I waited, convinced we'd need to break up a fight when they finally started talking. Two hours later, they walked out with smiles on their faces, and they have been meeting there every other week since.

"What do you think?" Tyler's voice comes from behind me as he wraps himself around my back.

"I can't believe you did this for me," I say. "The center doesn't even open for another six months."

"I know that," he says as his warmth leaves my back. I turn to see him kneeling down next to me. My hand flies to my mouth and tears fall from my eyes before I can even think.

"Claire, from the minute I saw you across the bar waving at me, you had every ounce of my attention. I had never seen anyone like you in my entire life. You taught me so many things in such a short time. Compassion, strength, forgiveness," he says, locking eyes with Jake for a second before coming back to mine. "Before you, I was alive, but I hadn't really lived for a long time. You pushed me to live. I can never thank you enough for that. In the last year, I have watched you do the same thing for so many other people. I know how special you are. I want to spend every second of the rest of my life watching you do amazing things. Claire Elizabeth Andrews, will you marry me?"

I fling myself down into his arms, almost knocking him over.

I nod my head yes, unable to form words over the tears running down my face. He slides the ring over my finger, and I grab his face in my hands. Staring at the man that picked up all of my broken pieces and somehow found a way to unbreak me.

About the Author

C.A. Grieco is a stay at home mama, that spends her days homeschooling her three kiddos, helping take care of the mini farm they have. She is married to her best friend; he was her love at first sight, and the reason she believes true love really exists. When she is not writing love stories, she is most likely lost in someone else's book or enjoying the beauty of nature on a hike.

Facebook: C.A. Grieco Romance author
Tiktok: @c.a.griecoauthor
Instagram: C.A. Grieco Author

Author note

To my readers,

I can not thank you all enough for taking the time to read my book. You are amazing!

I originally wrote this story over seven years ago with my newborn baby tucked in on my chest and a toddler on my lap. I wanted to wrap the heartbreaks of life with the beauty of love. Showing that through the darkest times there is a light ahead.

After I finished, I never thought I would open it again. Years later, my amazing husband pushed me to pursue my dream of becoming an author. Many rewrites and edits later here we are.

Some may feel the characters fall in love too quickly, but I am an author that believes in love at first sight. Mostly because I am living it. I met my husband during my darkness. Fell head over heels damn near instantly. He is my light, and over the last twelve years, we have continued to pick that candle up for each other to fight through it all.

I hope one day you believe in that kind of love, too.

Acknowledgments

To my children. I wouldn't be half of the woman I am without you pushing me every day to be the best version of myself. I hope me facing my fears teaches you guys to face all of yours. I want you to live fearless, epic lives that make you so very happy.

To my husband, you are my freaking rock. You have stood by my side for every second of this journey. Reading, helping me edit, wiping my tears, and pulling me to my feet when I felt like I wasn't enough.

To my family, you have listened to me talk about this book for years and never doubted I would get here. I truly believe I have the best family ever!

To my best friend, If I never met you my life would suck. You are my soul sister and I am forever grateful you are in my life. Thank you for always being there for me and all the help on this book.

To my editor, you pushed me to make this book better. I am forever thankful for that!

Made in the USA
Middletown, DE
13 March 2024